"I WON'T KEEP YOU FOR LONG, JUANITA," FARGO TOLD HER.

"Thank you for saving me from those two men. The other girls told me about them. They are animals. I did not want to go with them," she said softly, stepping out of her skirt. Her chemise and slip went next and she stood before him, naked, her long dark hair flowing.

"Juanita," Fargo started to explain, feeling the quickening in his loins as he gazed upon her. "I did not take you from those two so I could have you for myself. I just wanted to help."

"I know that, Skye." She moved up onto the bed beside him. "But you have all your teeth. You have shoulders as wide as a barn door. You do not smell like manure, and you have eyes as blue as lake water. Besides, you are one fine gentleman. So now I thank you," she said, easing her silken body onto his, ending his protest with her lips. . . .

Exciting Westerns by Jon Sharpe

THE BADGE

by
Jon Sharpe

A SIGNET BOOK

NEW AMERICAN LIBRARY

NAL BOOKS ARE AVAILABLE AT QUANTITY DISCOUNTS
WHEN USED TO PROMOTE PRODUCTS OR SERVICES.
FOR INFORMATION PLEASE WRITE TO PREMIUM MARKETING DIVISION,
NEW AMERICAN LIBRARY, 1633 BROADWAY,
NEW YORK, NEW YORK 10019.

The first chapter of this book appeared in *Kiowa Kill*,
the thirty-fifth volume in this series.

SIGNET TRADEMARK REG. U.S. PAT. OFF. AND FOREIGN COUNTRIES
REGISTERED TRADEMARK—MARCA REGISTRADA
HECHO EN CHICAGO, U.S.A.

SIGNET, SIGNET CLASSIC, MENTOR, PLUME, MERIDIAN AND NAL BOOKS
are published by New American Library,
1633 Broadway, New York, New York 10019

First Printing, December, 1984

1 2 3 4 5 6 7 8 9

PRINTED IN THE UNITED STATES OF AMERICA

The Trailsman

Beginnings . . . they bend the tree and they mark the man. Skye Fargo was born when he was eighteen. Terror was his midwife, vengeance his first cry. Killing spawned Skye Fargo, ruthless, cold-blooded murder. Out of the acrid smoke of gunpowder still hanging in the air, he rose, cried out a promise never forgotten.

The Trailsman, they began to call him all across the West, searcher, scout, hunter, the man who could see where others only looked, his skills for hire but not his soul, the man who lived each day to the fullest, yet trailed each tomorrow. Skye Fargo, the Trailsman, the seeker who could take the wildness of a land and the wanting of a woman and make them his own.

*1861. Deep in Crow country,
where moonshine and blood set off
the drums of war . . .*

1

Skye Fargo sat quietly beside Marshal Wolf Caulder on the veranda of Pierce's only hotel. The two men had tipped their chairs back against the wall and were resting with their ankles crossed on the hotel's porch railing. Across the street squatted the Wells Fargo express office. A gold-mining boomtown high in the snow-tipped peaks of Idaho, Pierce's Market Street was nearly empty as the pitiless, midsummer sun poured down on the raw buildings.

A big man, over six feet tall, Fargo had a thick head of raven-black hair that reached to his massive, powerful shoulders. He was dressed in buckskins and a tan wide-brimmed hat, which he had tipped forward over his forehead to shield his eyes from the sun's glare. Reaching to the floor of the veranda, Fargo lifted a fifth of whiskey to his mouth and pulled on it. Beside him, Wolf Caulder lit a cigarette.

At the moment the two men were discussing the preposterous dime novels of Erasmus Beadle, of which more than a dozen were available in the hotel lobby.

"Hard to believe anyone would believe that crap," remarked Caulder. The marshal wore a black, flat-crowned stetson, a clean white cotton shirt under his vest, and faded Levi's tucked into scuffed half-boots. He was a tall, lean man with a crooked tilt to his wide shoulders and a black patch that covered his right eye. A long, puckered scar ran back from his right eye socket to his ear, imparting to that side of his face a crushed, bent look.

"What did you think of Grizzly Bill, that dude who was supposed to 've killed a grizzly with a kitchen knife?" Fargo asked, his hawklike eyes snapping with amusement.

"A real hero, he was—and don't forget that was just after he wiped out a tribe of Sioux with a single six-shooter."

"And of course he never had to reload it."

Caulder chuckled. "Just put it between covers, I guess. That's all it takes to make some people believe just about anything."

"Especially Eastern dudes."

"Trouble is, some of them dudes come west to try their hand at killin' redskins and buffalo."

Fargo shook his head in mild wonderment at the foolishness of some mortals and watched idly as four men finished crossing the street and mounted the porch steps leading into the Wells Fargo office. A moment later, he glanced up the street and saw a dust-laden rider leading four saddled mounts down Market Street.

"Now, why would that jasper be leading four saddled horses into town, do you think?" Fargo asked softly.

Caulder did not answer, but it was obvious he was exploring the same possibility as Fargo. Frowning, Caulder pushed his chair gently forward, the wooden legs coming down without a sound onto the porch. He flicked his cigarette into the baked dust of Market Street and stood up. Fargo pushed his chair forward also, but he remained sitting in it as the two of them watched the approaching rider. The horseman appeared to be leading those four horses directly toward the express office.

"I see what you mean," Caulder said softly to Fargo. "Maybe you better stay here and keep your ass down."

Caulder removed the marshal's badge from his vest and dropped it into his pocket. Fargo understood the move at once. Caulder wanted to get across the street and into that express office without alerting the rider to the fact that he was a law officer. Snugging his hat down more firmly, Caulder descended the veranda steps and started across the street. For a moment Fargo watched Caulder go. Then he got to his feet and left the veranda to follow him.

Gaining the wooden sidewalk in front of Seth Mabry's barbershop, Fargo kept behind Caulder as the marshal continued on toward the express office. A covey of snaggle-toothed whores swept out of Luke's Saloon and began giggling when they saw Fargo approaching. Fargo solemnly touched the brim of his hat to the soiled doves as he continued to follow Caulder.

The horseman was still leading the four saddled mounts down the street toward the express office, and now he was only a few stores down from it. Assuming those four men who had just entered Wells Fargo were holding it up, Fargo knew that the marshal was anxious to collar them in the office before they charged out with guns blazing. In the enusing gunfire, innocent townspeople could easily get cut down.

Fargo hung back, his right hand resting on his gun butt as Caulder mounted the steps and entered the Wells Fargo office. For long minutes nothing happened. Fargo was beginning to relax, almost convinced that their fears had been groundless, the product of a lazy afternoon after having read too many of Beadle's dime novels.

The sudden crash of gunfire told him differently.

Guns blazing, four outlaws broke from the office and bolted down the steps to their mounts, bulky saddlebags slung over their shoulders. Pulling up, Fargo drew his Colt and got off a quick shot, catching the brim of an outlaw's hat and snapping it off his head. The five outlaws turned their guns on Fargo. The fire was heavy enough and one bullet caught Fargo high on the left shoulder, slamming him backward.

He scrambled into the cover of a nearby doorway. Still shooting, the outlaws mounted up and galloped out of town. Ignoring his shoulder wound, Fargo flung a couple of futile shots after them, then dashed up the stairs and into the express office.

Wolf Caulder was lying in a pool of his own blood, the distraught Wells Fargo clerk bending over him. When Fargo leaned close, he saw that Caulder was gut-shot. It was not a pretty sight.

"Son of a bitch," Caulder whispered to Fargo. "That was Johnny Ringo! An old sidekick."

"And he shot you?"

Caulder nodded, grinning crookedly.

"I think I recognize one of those men," Fargo told Caulder. "Who were the others?"

"Don't know."

By this time miners and townsmen had crowded into the tiny office, those behind jostling the men in front as they tried to get a better view of the wounded marshal. Fargo looked up to see the doctor pushing his way through their ranks, using his black bag as a kind of battering ram. Waving Fargo aside, he bent swiftly to examine Caulder's wound. Then he looked up at the four closest men and told them to bring Caulder over to the saloon. He would have to operate on one of the gaming tables.

Caulder was lifted and carried none too gently out of the express office. Fargo followed at a distance, his head reeling, a deadly fatigue falling over his limbs. His shoulder wound was causing him to lose considerable blood, and he knew he should get it tended to as soon as possible. But all he could think of at the moment was taking after Johnny Ringo—and the stocky outlaw that rode with him.

There were just two more for Sky Fargo to find—and that outlaw he had spotted with Ringo could be one of them.

* * *

13

Later that night Fargo sat a lonely vigil beside the long, silent figure of Wolf Caulder as he lay unconscious on his bed. Caulder did not look good. His color had faded completely. The eye patch had been taken off by the doctor and no one had bothered to replace it.

As Fargo gazed into the awful, puckered hole where the marshal's eye should have sat, he wondered how the man could have sustained such a terrible wound. Not that it mattered any longer. Though the doctor had pushed what was left of Caulder's intestines back into his abdomen and sewn him up, he held little hope for the marshal's survival. He told Fargo that Caulder would be lucky to make it through the night.

After he took care of Caulder, the doctor had repaired Fargo's shoulder. The bullet had torn up considerable muscle and nipped an artery. The result was a loss of blood that had left Fargo as weak as a kitten.

Caulder stirred. "Water," he said, his voice barely above a whisper.

Fargo filled a glass from a pitcher sitting on the night table and lifted Caulder's head so he could drink from the glass. Caulder gulped the water gratefully, then coughed most of it back up.

Fargo put the glass back on the table and leaned close. "Caulder, tell me what happened in that office."

"I walked in and saw Ringo," Caulder whispered softly. "I was surprised. It really stopped me. I didn't keep my gun on them. I let it drop. Ringo smiled. He seemed glad to see me."

14

"Then he gut-shot you."

"He turned bad, Fargo. Real bad. He's finished me, looks like."

"Hell, Caulder. You ain't dead yet. The doc got the bullet out and he's sewed you up good and proper."

"You know better than that, Fargo. No bullshit, okay?"

"Okay, wolf. No bullshit. You got any idea where this Ringo jasper might be headin'?"

"For the past week I been hearin' things . . . there's a town in the mountains south of here."

Fargo leaned closer. "Where?"

"Big Rock . . . Lost River Range."

Fargo sat back, frowning. He knew the Lost River country. And he had heard of Big Rock.

"Fargo," Caulder whispered hoarsely. A cold sweat had broken out on his forehead. "Get Ringo and the rest of them bastards for me, will you?"

Fargo did not hesitate. "I'll do what I can, Caulder. That's a promise."

"Take my badge, Fargo. It's in my pocket."

Fargo remembered seeing Caulder pocket his badge before leaving the veranda. He reached into the man's pocket and withdrew the badge.

"I got it, Caulder."

"I'm deputizin' you, Fargo. That'll make it all nice and legal."

"Sure, Caulder. But I would have gone after them anyway, I'm thinking."

"Hell, I knew that," Caulder said, a faint smile creasing his ravaged face. Then he closed his eyes. A moment later, his broken visage seemed to cave in slightly and his long body stretched out. Fargo took a deep breath, then stood up and looked for a moment down at the man who had lowered his gun at sight of an old friend. And was now a dead man as a result.

Fargo pinned on the badge and left the room.

A week later Skye Fargo rode slowly into Big Rock astride his handsome Ovaro pinto. His shoulder wound had forced him to spend longer than he wished in Pierce, and at the moment the wound was forcing him to let his pinto pick his own gait. As he rode, he kept the brim of his hat low enough to shield his eyes from the sun's glare. Ahead of him he saw a weathered huddle of buildings crouched in amid the towering peaks of the Lost River Range.

A plank bridge carried him across the creek into the town. For a while he rode beside empty single-story frame houses, their curtainless windows coated with dust. Soon he came to the row of false-front buildings on both sides of the street that made up the town's business district. Another road cut south out of the foothills to form an intersection ahead of him. On the four corners sat a hotel, a general store, and two large saloons. Across from the hotel, Fargo saw the livery stable, and headed for it.

Easing his pinto to a halt in front of the livery, Fargo dismounted carefully. An old man materialized out of the stable's gloom, his cheek swollen with tobacco.

"Second stall back," he told Fargo, loosing a black darter to the ground beside him.

Fargo gave the pinto a small drink at the street trough first, then led him into the stall, where he removed the saddle. Leaving the stable, he lugged his saddle and all the rest of his gear across the street to the hotel. There was a room with tubs on the first floor in back. After he had taken advantage of this luxury, he ate in the hotel's cramped dining room, then drifted through the lobby into the hotel's elaborate saloon.

Taking a seat at a table in the far corner, he sipped his beer and kept his eye on the flipping batwings. They were seldom still. From the look of the saloon's customers, it was obvious that most of the men were on the dodge—which was one very good reason why Fargo had decided to keep his badge in his pocket. The saloon was noisy enough and there was no lack of poker tables or women.

Fargo kept his eyes open, hoping to catch sight of Ringo or any of his gang. Pretty sure he would know Ringo when he saw him, he was not too discouraged when after more than two hours, neither Ringo nor any of his gang members showed up. He would just have to be patient. If Ringo's gang wanted a town to celebrate a heist, this was it. And if he had been and gone, Fargo would soon find that out easily enough.

Six percentage girls worked the place, all of them obviously shipped up from Mexico, judging from their olive complexions, their dark, sorrowful eyes, and long black hair hanging past their shoulders. The hotel saloon's owner was too cheap to provide the girls with any fancy spangled dresses, but what they wore was low enough in front and high enough above the ankles to make up for that lack.

The girls seemed reasonably content with their lot, except for one of them, who kept strictly to business, which appeared to be waiting on the customers at their tables. Nevertheless, taller than the other girls, with more meat on her bones, she seemed an irresistible attraction to the older, more grizzled patrons. As the evening wore on and she found herself more and more manhandled, the proud angry light in her eyes flared more openly.

At last, unable to witness the cuffing and casual brutality the girl was being forced to endure, Fargo paid his tab and returned to the hotel lobby. His long ride that day had tired him considerably, and in addition, his shoulder was beginning to ache like a sore tooth. He was eager to get up to his room so he could tend to it.

He asked the desk clerk for his room key. As the clerk reached for it, Fargo heard a sharp scuffle behind him. He turned. The tall bar girl was being hauled roughly past the desk by two older men. Their yellow teeth gleamed wolfishly through their tobacco-stained beards. A small fat man—the hotel owner—rushed out of his office behind the desk and tried to talk the two men out of taking the girl upstairs.

But the two men would have none of it.

They were obviously miners. Their boots were heavy with mud. Their faces and hands were almost black from weeks of pawing in the bowels of the earth. They stank. The one closest to Fargo was the tallest—a lean, raw-faced man with sick, furtive eyes.

"Now lookee here, Pablo," he was telling the

hotel owner, "Sam and me, we been steady customers this past year and we always pay up. We know what you're doin'. You're saving up this here Mex for yerself."

"Slim, that ees not true," the hotel owner cried.

"Never mind that," Slim replied. "We'll pay you double tonight. And all of it in gold dust. So leave us be!"

"No," Pablo said. "You go back in the saloon. I'll send Dolores to your table. She'll be down soon. Juanita, here, she no want to go upstairs with you two."

"Now, what the hell difference does that make?"

Sam spoke up then. He was a bit unsteady on his feet as he held the girl's waist in a viselike grip. "We don't want Dolores. It's like screwin' a rain barrel. This here Juanita suits us fine." Sam grinned at her. " 'Bout time she got broke in real good and proper."

Slim reached over and grabbed a fistful of Juanita's buttocks and squeezed. The girl made a tiny cry. The two men burst into laughter. The smaller one hauled the girl toward the stairs, Slim following. Fargo saw that Pablo was wavering. The man was obviously unwilling to go against the wishes of the two men. On the other hand, he seemed to care greatly for Juanita and did not want these men to have her.

Fargo thrust his room key into his pocket, then caught the girl's eye—and winked. It was not a playful wink, but one designed to alert the girl to his intentions. Then he moved ahead of the two men and positioned himself before them at the foot of the stairs.

"Hey, Juanita," he cried, pulling the girl out of the startled Slim's grasp and into his own arms. "I just got in. I told you I'd be here tonight. How come you're with these two?"

"Hey!" protested Sam. "Who're you?"

"Hold it right there, mister," Slim said. "She's with us!"

Ignoring Sam, Fargo tucked his arm around Juanita's waist and leaned close. Into her ears he whispered, "Play along! My name's Skye Fargo!"

Juanita smiled brilliantly. "Skye!" she cried. "Where have you been? I have wait so long for you."

Patting Juanita on the ass, he sent her up the stairs ahead of him. But the two miners were not deceived. They knew what Fargo was doing and they were furious at his intervention.

Reaching out, Slim grabbed Fargo's right arm and spun him about. "You ain't foolin' me, you son of a bitch! I ain't gonna let you—"

That was all he got out. Fargo backhanded Slim across his cheek. The man went reeling back against the wall. Sam took a step back and clawed for his gun. But Fargo's own six-gun was out well ahead of the half-soused miner. Before Sam could bring up his weapon, Fargo brought the barrel of his Colt down hard on the smaller man's wrist. The six-gun clattered to the floor.

"*Señor!*"

It was the girl. Fargo whirled. Slim was charging him. Holstering his Colt, Fargo ducked aside and caught the man as he reeled past him. With both hands Fargo propelled the man headfirst into the wall. Slim shook himself groggily, then turned and rushed back at Fargo. Fargo waited, then drove his fist into the man's face, crunching into his nose. Slim's head snapped back, a heavy freshet of blood streaming from one nostril. Fargo drove in closer and caught Slim about his head and shoulders in a furious, sledging flurry that drove Slim out of the lobby and into the saloon.

As Slim disappeared through the doorway and crashed out of sight to the floor, an immediate silence fell over the saloon. Fargo waited for Slim to pick himself up and reappear in the doorway. He did not. Fargo turned back to the other miner. Sam had sunk to the floor, holding on to his swollen wrist. His Colt was lying at his feet, but he made no effort to reach for it.

Fargo turned to the girl. "My room is at the head of the stairs," he told her.

She turned and hurried up the flight ahead of him. Without looking back at the miner or the hotel owner, Fargo followed the girl up the stairs and into his room.

2

Fargo closed the door. Juanita's face was alive with gratitude.

"Thank you, *señor*," she cried. "Thank you!"

"That's all right, Juanita," Fargo assured her. "And don't worry. I won't keep you long." He moved past her to the bed and sank wearily down onto it. "Just stay here for a few minutes—until those two find someone else."

Juanita moved quickly across the room to him. "Those two men, they are animals. The other girls, they tell me about them." She shuddered. "I do not want to go with them."

"Who are they?"

"I know only that they have a mine somewhere in the mountains. It is well-hidden, I hear."

Fargo nodded, then looked away from Juanita. He was suddenly preoccupied with the unusual discomfort in his shoulder. It was worse than it had been in the saloon. Earlier, when he had taken his bath, he had noticed how raw the area around the stitches in his shoulder had grown. Now the wound seemed warm and heavy with fresh blood and it occurred to him that the stitches might have ripped out during that sudden flurry of activity downstairs.

"Excuse me, Juanita," he said to the girl as he carefully shrugged out of his shirt, exposing the blood-soaked bandage.

At sight of it, Juanita uttered a small cry and moved quickly closer and slowly began to unwind the dressing. Her fingers were deft and gentle. Fargo leaned back against the head of the bed and let her work. As soon as the bandage was removed, Fargo looked closely and felt considerably relieved. Though a great deal of blood had oozed through the sutures, they appeared to be holding.

Juanita got to her feet. "I come back soon," she told him. "You stay quiet. Please."

Fargo was in no mood to argue. He placed his Colt under the pillow, then lay down on the bed, his head resting on it, as Juanita hurried from the room. He closed his eyes and dozed for a short while until Juanita hurried in sometime later with a pan of steaming water, fresh bandages, and an enormous bar of yellow soap.

"I will clean it for you," she told him as she placed the pan down on the dresser beside his bed. "You will see. It is a very ugly wound. But I do good with gunshots."

And she did.

She did not hesitate to cause him pain as she cleansed the area around the wound itself. The yellow soap stung, but that fact comforted him. When she rebandaged it, the dressing was firm, supportive, yet not unduly tight. Fargo gingerly lifted his shoulder, then flexed it. It felt much better.

He leaned back against the head of the bed and smiled gratefully at Juanita. "Very good. It feels much better."

Pleased, she pulled off his boots, then began unbuttoning his pants. He started to tell her it was unnecessary, but thought better of it and let her deft, warm fingers peel them off. In a monent he lay naked on the bed before her. She uttered a barely audible gasp when she saw the bear-claw scar in the shape of a half-moon on his forearm and took a good look at the powerful, ridged muscles standing out on his massive shoulders.

Reaching out, she brushed his unruly black hair—the color of a raven's wing—back off his forehead. "I think you must have Indian blood, Skye."

He chuckled. "True, Juanita—on my mother's side. But don't worry. I won't scalp you."

"No," she said softly, stepping out of her skirt, "I do not think so." Her chemise and slip went next and she stood before him naked, her long dark hair flowing down past her buttocks, her pubic patch gleaming darkly.

"Juanita," Fargo told her, feeling the quickening in his loins as she gazed upon her, "I did not take you from those two so I could have you for myself. I just wanted to help."

"I know that, Skye," she said, moving up onto the bed beside him. "But you have all your teeth. You have shoulders as wide as a barn door. You do not smell like the cow manure or horse manure, and you have eyes as blue as lake water. Besides, you are one fine gentleman." She snuggled her long olive figure against Fargo's pale nakedness. "So now I thank you."

Easing her silken smooth body up onto his, she slipped her long legs over his torso. He kissed her on her warm, responsive lips, then fastened his mouth to her breasts, his tongue flicking at her erect nipples while his hands explored her completely—but always gently.

Only when at last she began to moan aloud and grabbed a fistful of his hair, threatening to scalp him without the aid of a knife, did he roll slowly over and carefully spread her thighs and ease himself up onto her. He teased her at first with the tip of his erection, pulling back twice.

Juanita gasped. "You are one devil, Skye," she cried. "You drive this woman wild! Please! Do not play with me any longer."

He smiled down at her. "I'll see what I can do."

He was mildly disappointed at the ease with which he penetrated her. So moist had she become as a result of his foreplay that at first he could barely feel the walls of her muff closing about his erection. But at once she tightened on him like a powerful fist, and he felt himself swell magnificently. With deep, measured thrusts, he began to probe her warm depths. With each thrust, he heard her gasp in pleasure. Laughing happily, she reached up to pull him to her, thrusting her buttocks up to meet each downward thrust.

Before long, Fargo found himself mounting inexorably to his climax. Grunting happily, he felt Juanita's arms tightening around his neck. He buried his face in her neck and began driving even harder. Soon, throwing aside all restraint, he swept past the point of no return. He heard Juanita's gasps, then her sharp, inarticulate cries. At one point he thought Juanita was screaming, but he paid no attention as he continued to pound at her with a grim, battering intensity.

Abruptly lifting her legs, Juanita tightened her ankles behind his back, enclosing Fargo's waist in a viselike grip that pulled him still deeper into her. Fargo pushed up onto his elbows and gazed down at her as he continued to thrust. Grunting furiously, Juanita began to move her head back and forth. Then she came, uttering a long, low moan that rose to a high scream just as Fargo reached his own shattering climax, his engorged erection pulsing wildly into her tightening, gyrating muff.

Feeling pleasantly spent, he rolled off her. She rested her head on his shoulder and kissed him lightly on the face. Then the lips. He reached over and pulled her closer. Her hand dropped to his crotch.

"Oh, my," she said. "You are still so big."

"I don't believe it," he said, kissing her on the mouth, his tongue reaching deeply into her.

"I do," she replied impishly, thrusting herself against him.

He reached down to feel her warm moistness. Gently, he stroked her silky pubic mound. Then he caught one of her breasts with his lips and began tugging at it with his tongue, smothering it with his lips. At last her head fell back. Deep, sobbing gasps broke from her taut throat as she let the joy of it take her completely. Lost in it, her entire body trembling, she gave a final cry and went limp in his arms.

Fargo lifted his lips from her breast and kissed her on the mouth deeply.

"The other breast, Skye," she cried. "Please."

He obeyed her and at the same time rolled over onto her again and thrust himself into her. She sighed and flung both arms around his neck. He began pumping then, violently, his mouth still holding her breast. This time she met each thrust of his with one of her own, her own violence matching his perfectly. Her feverish trembling began much sooner than before, but that was all right with Fargo. He, too, was rapidly reaching a peak. Releasing her breast, he lunged fiercely, pinning her to the bed and driving in so far he heard her gasp in a sudden, frightening cry of delight. Faster and faster he rocked, racing Juanita to her climax—until he surpassed her and, with one mighty, triumphant thrust, slipped over the edge.

He held himself deep, pumping wildly within her, listening to Juanita's tiny cries of delight as she, too, came, and came—and came. At last his own involuntary thrusting subsided, and this time, spent completely, he rolled off her and sprawled on his back. He glanced over at her. She was still on her back, her face glistening with perspiration. She had flung one arm over her eyes. Her mouth was partly open, her tongue sliding back and forth across her upper lip—as if she had eaten something incomparably delicious and was still savoring it

"Juanita," he said after a decent interval, "I am

looking for five men. They would have ridden here with lots of gold dust."

She lifted her head to look at him. "Are you a lawman?"

"Not exactly. But I have a badge. And I want those men."

"I have seen the men you seek," she told him softly. "I will tell you all I know."

She told him then of five men who had entered Big Rock four days before. They had taken rooms in this hotel and proceeded to pay generously for whatever they wanted. One of them—a man called Murdo—played poker and faro almost around the clock, and lost great amounts of gold dust without complaint. The others had preferred to stay in their room with a woman—all except their leader. This one was a restless, surly man who brought fear into Juanita's eyes as she recalled him.

"Johnny Ringo?" Fargo prodded quietly. "Was that his name?"

Juanita nodded. "Yes," she said, her voice suddenly cold. "He was a devil, that one. He beat Dolores."

"Badly?"

"She will be all right. Ringo paid Pablo and Dolores for his unkindness when he sobered up. He had much gold dust, that one."

"That gold dust was stolen, Juanita."

Juanita nodded, her large dark eyes thoughtful. "Sí, we all knew they must have robbed some place to have all that gold dust. But we hear of no robbery near here."

Fargo nodded. "They held up an express office

many miles north of here in Pierce, near that gold strike."

"That is very far from here."

"Yes."

"And still you chase them?"

Fargo nodded and leaned his head back on the pillow. "Yes. Still I chase them. They left a good friend of mine dead. Are they still here?"

"No. They leave two days ago."

Fargo nodded. For now he had no more questions. That he was still this close to Ringo gave him heart. He had come a long way. And he still had farther to go. But he had no doubt he would catch up to Ringo now. Meanwhile, he was finding it difficult to carry on the conversation. He had been bone-tired when he climbed the stairs to his room. For a while Juanita had made him forget that. But no longer was he able to fight back the enormous fatigue that sat like anvils upon his eyelids and limbs. He smiled weakly at Juanita.

"I think I am going to fall asleep any minute, Juanita," he told her. "Maybe you'd better get on back downstairs."

"Sí," she said, sitting up and smiling down at him. "I am afraId I have tire you out."

"I wasn't complaining, Juanita."

"I know," she said, leaning close and kissing him lightly on the forehead. She pulled the covers up over his naked body.

As the cool sheets fell over him, Fargo closed his eyes and dropped into an exhausted sleep.

A cannon went off under his bed. Or that was how

it sounded. Fargo came awake in an instant and jumped out of bed. In the pale light of dawn he saw no one. He was alone in his room.

The silence was broken by the scuffle of footsteps outside his door, startled shouts, and the sound of a man crying out in rage and panic. Reaching for the Colt he had placed under his pillow, he padded swiftly across the room and flung open the door. The hallway was thick with an acrid pall of gunpowder, and standing resolutely by his door—an overturned chair behind her—was Juanita. An enormous Colt was still clutched in her hands.

Fargo swung his gaze to the stairwell. Slim's dirty face was just ducking below the floor level. A neat hole stared at him from the wall above the landing. It was where Juanita's bullet had gone. Since she had fired only once, Fargo knew Juanita had missed Slim.

But she had sure as hell scared him off—and for that Fargo was grateful.

He reached down and righted the overturned chair. Then he smiled at Juanita. "Thank you," he told her.

Her face was chalk-white. But her jaw was set with iron resolve. As a sudden flurry of footsteps began pounding up the stairs, Juanita pushed Fargo gently back into his room and closed the door behind them.

"You are naked, Skye," she told him, her eyes alight suddenly.

"So I am," he admitted. He moved back to the bed and pulled on his long johns. "Were you out there all night?"

"Yes. But I fell asleep, Skye," she said with genuine bitterness. "I am so sorry."

"Hell, Juanita. You got no cause to feel bad. You did fine."

"The board on the top step, it squeaked. I open my eyes and see Slim. He is almost to the door. I was so crazy with surprise, I pulled the trigger without I aim."

Fargo laughed, pulling on his britches. "That's all right, Juanita. It is a good thing you didn't aim. You might have killed the son of a bitch. And you wouldn't like the blood of any man on your conscience."

She thrust her Colt into her skirt pocket. "Maybe, Skye. But that man Slim, he is one bad devil."

"Last night you said Johnny Ringo and his men left two days ago. That right, Juanita?"

She nodded.

"Which way'd they go? South?"

"No. Not South. They rode northeast through Pine Notch." She pointed out the window, indicating the direction they took. "I watched them ride out. Pablo and I were burying the one Ringo killed. They saw us as they rode by. Yet they did not even stop." Juanita shook her head at this lack of compassion. Then she looked with sudden concern into Fargo's face. "You must be careful of these men. They are all devils, I think."

He smiled at her concern. "You must promise, Juanita, not to tell anyone here that I'm after Ringo. I'm sure he has many friends here—with all that gold dust he threw around."

"I will tell no one," she said, her dark eyes steady.

"That's good, Juanita."

"And now I must go down and help Pablo in the kitchen." She smiled. "And he will want to know about that shot, I think."

He watched her proud figure stride from the room. Then he sat back down on his bed and reached for his boots. His shoulder, he noted with some satisfaction, was feeling much better.

Not long after, Fargo arrived downstairs with his gear and found an empty table in the dining room. Dropping his gear in an empty chair, he looked up and saw Juanita, already serving as a waitress, hurrying over to his table, a smile on her face.

"Do you think Pablo would let me have breakfast with you?" Fargo asked her.

His question took her by surprise. "I do not know," she told him, blushing. She glanced back as Pablo appeared in the kitchen doorway.

Fargo beckoned to him.

Pablo hurried over, smiling nervously at Fargo. "Is everything all right, *señor*?"

"Juanita spent the night on a chair outside my door. And it's a good thing she did. One of your guests came after me. I'd like Juanita to join me for breakfast."

"Of course, *señor*!" he said. "It is me who must thank you for saving Juanita from those two men!"

There was no more discussion and Juanita sat down at the table. Fargo ordered for both of them. When the breakfast arrived, he found she ate with an impressive display of manners. Her banter was light, and more than once she had Fargo laughing outright. There was more—much more—to this young Mexican girl than Fargo would have guessed at first glance.

When he had finished breakfast, Fargo pushed aside his plate, reached for coffee, and waved the hotel owner over to the table. Pablo hurried over at once.

"Sit down, Pablo," Fargo said.

The little man pulled over a chair and sat down, glancing nervously at Juanita as he did so.

"I don't want any reprisals for what Juanita did outside my door this morning," Fargo told the man. "There ain't too much law visible in this town. That means she just might have saved my life." He dug into his pocket and pulled out two double eagles. "There's a bullet hole in the wall upstairs. That should take care of any damage."

Pablo's eyes went large. "That is more than enough, *señor*. Thank you! Juanita is a good girl. I did not want her to go with those two. She is not like the other girls." As he spoke, he reached over and patted Juanita on her arm, his dark eyes glowing with pride.

"I agree, Pablo," Fargo said, getting to his feet.

"Are you going now?" Juanita asked.

Fargo nodded.

"Your shoulder, is it better?"

"It feels fine."

Impulsively, Juanita got to her feet, took Fargo's face in her hands, and pulled him close so she could

33

kiss him. Then she turned and darted from the dining room.

Fargo watched her go, aware of a sharp and sudden sense of loss. Then he shrugged at his own foolishness, said good-bye to Pablo, and strode from the hotel.

He had a long ride yet. But now he knew for sure which way Johnny Ringo was going—not south as he would have expected, but northeast, through Pine Notch.

And they were now only three days ahead of him.

3

Four days later, close to sunset, Fargo came upon a recent campsite. It looked to be about a week old. He dismounted to inspect the area more closely and almost at once caught sight of the spent cartridge casings. They were scattered about the campfire's dead embers, all of them within a relatively small circle.

One man had stood in front of the fire, firing his Colt.

A search over the rest of the campsite revealed only one more spent jacket. This one was close to where a rope tether had been sliced through. The spooked horses on the other side of the rope had left in a considerable panic, judging from the way the ground was torn up and from the horses' long strides.

Fargo eased himself back against a man-sized boulder and looked once more around the campsite. A picture was forming in his mind. The horses had been driven off by one man. That much was certain. And whoever had discovered what was happening—it could have been Ringo or any of the other members of his gang—had come awake in a hurry and started throwing lead at the one responsible. If Ringo and his men had been unable to retrieve those horses, they'd be afoot, chasing after the fellow who had taken their gold as well as their mounts.

The thieves had fallen out, it appeared.

Fargo pushed himself away from the boulder and started looking for footprints leaving the campsite. He found them soon enough. A set of four. They were on foot, then—four of them at least. And they appeared to be tracking the gang member who had taken their horses. Of course all this meant delay. A startling thought occurred to Fargo. He was assuming the gang member who had taken the horses was not Ringo. But suppose it was? Maybe Ringo had decided to take all of the remaining gold dust for himself.

Fargo shrugged. It didn't matter. He would get them all eventually, and that included Johnny Ringo.

For a moment Fargo considered riding after them in the gathering darkness. He looked up at the sky. There were no clouds and there had been no rain for weeks. He could not follow signs in the dark, and if there was no rain that night, the footprints would be just as easy to follow the next morning. Besides, his pinto was about ready to give out on him.

He decided to make camp for the night and move out at dawn the next day.

It was late the following afternoon when Fargo rode out onto a ledge and looked down at the scruffy, cottonwood-shaded ranch buildings far below him in the valley.

By this time Fargo was aware that the three men on foot were following the blood spoor of a wounded rider. That flurry of shots back at the camp must have winged the poor son of a bitch who had been caught stampeding the horses. The ranch below would probably have looked pretty welcome to the wounded gunman. It would give him the cover he needed to nurse his wound and fight off his pursuers.

But the ranch appeared deserted.

The pole corral out behind the stable was empty of horses. For the past ten minutes or so not a single ranch hand had moved between the buildings. And no smoke curled out of the ranch house's chimney. Fargo watched for a while longer, then pulled the Ovaro back off the ledge and started down the narrow trail that led to the valley floor.

An hour later, after a cautious ride across the lush flats fronting the ranch, he splashed through a shallow stream and rode into the cotton woods shading the spread.

Once through them, he sat his horse awhile behind one particularly large tree and looked beyond it to the silent ranch house. The long, low cabin that served as the main house sat as still and quiet as a coffin. From somewhere in the branches above him came the hard chattering of a chipmunk. Chickens were clucking about in the thick grass around a small shed just behind the cabin. At last, when Fargo caught sight of a covey of bobwhites feeding on a patch of clover near the chimney, he realized that—for a moment at least—the ranch *was* deserted.

He broke from the cottonwoods and rode across the compound to the hitch rail in front of the cabin. Pulling the pinto up, he called, "Hello, the house!"

As he had expected, there was no response. He dismounted and went inside. The signs of a recent departure were everywhere. He noted the partially consumed pieces of a chair lying coldly in the fireplace, a large dark stain on the floor, the flyspecked dishes in the sink. The shelves over the sink had been stripped of anything of value to men on the trail.

From the look of the place, it had been cleaned out not too long ago—possibly the day before.

The sound of the bobwhites exploding in sudden panic caused Fargo to turn. A hulking shadow loomed in the doorway. Dodging instinctively to one side, Fargo threw himself to the floor as the roar of a shotgun filled the interior of the cabin. But the shot went wild, and before the stranger could fire again, Fargo flung himself at the man and drove him back out through the doorway. The shotgun detonated again, this time sending its charge harmlessly into the heavens. Fargo clubbed the man with his fist, the force of his blow sending the man reeling backward. His feet gave way under him and he collapsed onto his back.

Drawing his big Colt, Fargo cocked it and took careful aim at the man's head. The fellow looked dazedly up at Fargo and groaned. That was when Fargo noticed the matted blood just under his rib cage.

"Don't shoot!" the stranger managed.

"Why the hell not? You just tried to kill me."

"This is my place. Besides, I thought you was one of Ringo's men come back to get me."

Fargo holstered his Colt. "What do they call you?"

"Frank Compton."

"I'm Skye Fargo," Fargo replied, kneeling beside the fellow. His wound looked ugly and was slick with warm blood. Compton was in his early forties, his hair graying. There was a softness about him that did not impress Fargo. Compton looked like a man who would take the easy road whenever it offered—with no concern if it were honest or not, the kind always looking for the big break as he got deeper and deeper into a hole. Though Beadle's dime novels never mentioned it, this was the kind of four-flusher who usually ended up seeking his fortune in the Wild West.

"You got to help me," Compton said. "You got to go after them!"

"Them?"

"A gang! They was crazy! First one came by, wounded. He was the one who shot me. Then the others stormed in after him." He reached up and grabbed Fargo's arm. "Rose! They took my wife with them. You got to go after them. You got to get her back!"

"Later," Fargo said. "Later. Right now, I got you to look after."

Fargo helped the man into the cabin, then over to his bed. The man groaned and almost passed out as he hit the bed. Fargo pulled off Compton's

39

clothes and inspected the wound. A considerable hunk of flesh had been carried away by the slug, but he was a lucky man. A few inches lower and the bullet would have smashed through his pelvis.

But the wound was filthy and already festering.

Working swiftly, Fargo found some soap, heated water on the wood stove, and then cleaned the wound out thoroughly with the soap and water, working as Juanita had on his shoulder wound. Through it all, Compton moaned and howled pitiably, a commotion that did not make Fargo gentler. If anything, Fargo became a little rougher. If there was one thing he could not abide, it was the sound of a grown man howling in pain. Perhaps the Indians were right: a man who blubbered like that had no soul.

When he had finished cleaning out the wound and bandaging it, he drew the covers up over Compton and looked down at the man. His slack, pale face attempted a smile.

"Anything to drink in here?" Fargo inquired.

Compton nodded. "Under the sink."

Fargo found a half-empty earthen jug. Extracting a couple of greasy tin cups from a pile of dishes, he filled both cups with the pale-yellow moonshine and rejoined the wounded man. Compton lifted himself painfully and gulped down the drink, then handed the cup back to Fargo, his eyes pleading for more. Fargo finished his own cup, then refilled Compton's cup and his own. Then he put the jug down beside the bed, pulled up a wooden chair, and sat down.

"You mentioned Ringo before," he told Compton. "Tell me what happened here."

Compton told of a man calling himself Murdo Mackenzie who rode up to the cabin four days before. The man was driving four horses before him and was himself seriously wounded in the leg. Compton had wanted to drive the man off, but his wife would not have it and made Compton help Murdo off his horse and into the ranch house. She tended him—cleaned and dressed his wound and gave him food. And later that night, Murdo sterilized the blade of his bowie in the coal-oil lamp's flame and dug the bullet out of his leg, with Rose holding the lamp close for him.

The next morning, feeling much better, Murdo began throwing his weight around. By the end of the day, Compton found him going after his wife. When Compton called him on it, Murdo had tried to slice him with his bowie. Compton had fled the cabin to get the shotgun he had left in the barn. But he was shot by Murdo before he could get to it. Then, when his wife attempted to go after him, Murdo had dragged her back into the cabin. And soon after that, the gang on Murdo's trail showed up. They killed Murdo and stayed the night and most of the next day, while one of them took a wagon and went back after the saddles they had cached along the trail.

"While they were doing all this, what were you doing?" Fargo asked.

"I'd lost so much blood from my wound, I was too weak to do much. I knew I wasn't no match for them, so I hid near the river. They looked for me.

Two of them. But I kept low until they rode out the next day. When I saw they was takin' Rose, I left the river and ran after them.

"But they didn't even see me or hear me. I ran as far as I could. Then I just . . . collapsed. I guess I lost plenty of blood by that time and passed out again. When I awoke, it was pretty late. I got back to the barn and passed out again. When I came to this time, I saw your horse at the hitch rail and thought one of them had come back to finish me."

"What did Murdo tell you before they killed him?"

"He said he'd lost too much of his gold dust in Big Rock, so he just decided to help himself to the rest. He figured to kill Johnny Ringo in the bargain, but the son of a bitch woke up before he could."

Fargo nodded. Murdo's explanation jibed pretty well with what he had already figured from the signs around that campfire. "Which way are they headed?"

"Through White Horn Pass. Looked like they was headin' for Montana Territory."

"They're a full day's ride ahead of me, then."

"No, they're not. You can overtake them easy."

"How?"

"Go through the mountains and meet them on the other side of the pass. Just follow the riverbed till you get to the canyon. There's a trail over the canyon wall. Follow it."

"I'll have to ride through the riverbed?"

"That's the only way. You could never make it following the bank. But this time of the year, the water's only a couple of feet deep. It's fast, but you can make it. There's no other way through the mountains."

Fargo stood up. "I'll pull out first thing in the morning. Will you be all right here?"

"Sure. I'll be fine. You just get after them." He moved painfully and glanced at the jug sitting on the floor. "If those bastards had left any horseflesh, I'd go after them with you. I want Rose back."

"Get some sleep," Fargo told Compton, reaching down and handing him the jug.

Compton drank greedily, directly from the jug, wiped off his mouth with the back of his hand, then gave the jug back to Fargo. Fargo took the jug from him and put it back under the sink.

Then he went outside to tend to his pinto.

Fargo reached the canyon an hour after sunup, then put his pinto into the swift, clear water and started upstream. He found that Frank Campton's estimate of the stream's depth at this time of the year had been overly optimistic. In places the water reached a depth of at least four feet. His thighs were soon soaked, his boots heavy with moisture. On both sides of him, sheer walls of rock reared skyward, cutting off the sunlight almost completely. Before long, it turned into a wet, cold ride.

The Ovaro stumbled in the creek bed's smooth gravel. Fargo patted his neck and soothed him with soft words—and kept on. Compton had been right about the impossibility for anyone traveling along the stream's shore. There was no shore, actually. The stream had sliced its passage out of sheer rock.

A mountain goat would have had difficulty following the river channel's shoreline.

The water's rush increased as the slope of the streambed lifted. Each time he glanced up at the bright silver of the sky overhead, it seemed to have receded still farther from him. After a while he came to an abrupt turn and found himself moving over a small, frantic stretch of white water. The pinto snorted nervously and shook his head as he picked his way along. Fargo patted his neck, urging him on with gentle words.

About a mile into the canyon, the rapids fell away and the water became so smooth and clear that when he glanced down at the stream, it was as if he were looking through a pane of glass at the gravel resting in the streambed. The pines clinging to the slopes were smaller now and the great, perpendicular slabs of rock through which the stream had cut its way appeared to be leaning closer. He glanced up. The comforting strip of bright blue was no longer visible. The canyon walls had folded over, cutting off the sky entirely. It was as if he had moved imperceptibly underground. At the same time, he became aware of a distant roaring—like the murmur of wind in the tops of pines. The pinto carried him around a shoulder of rock and he saw ahead of him a mist rising from the stream. At the same time a dampness fell over him. He was approaching a waterfall.

He urged the pinto on. About twenty yards before the deep pool gouged out by the cataract, he glanced up at the thin plume of water that plunged down into the stream. The water came from such a height that by the time it was three-quarters of the way down, it was as delicate and lacy as a bridal veil.

Fargo looked away from the waterfall and caught sight of a trail leading out of the streambed. He nudged the pinto toward it and the pony clattered gratefully up onto the rocky trail. The trail looped steeply up the side of the canyon wall. The short switchback courses took Fargo higher and higher, and soon the stream he had left behind was no longer visible and the sound of the waterfall only a faint sighing whisper hanging in the air about him.

Some time past noon, he saw a mine entrance, dismounted, and made his noon camp. There was a thin stream nearby and a small patch of grass to one side of the mine entrance. Fargo dined on sourdough biscuits and jerky, rested awhile, then mounted up and went on. When night fell, he was still toiling up the canyon wall.

A chill night wind began to blow off the snow-clad summits above him. Abruptly, the trail dipped. Pleased at having reached the ridge and hoping soon to find himself over the mountain, he urged the pinto on, looking for a suitable campsite. But it was soon dark and Fargo could feel the trail dropping steeply ahead of him. From the feel of it, Fargo judged it had not recently been used and was possibly little more than a foothold cut out by deer and mountain goats.

He considered going back. But only for a moment. He would not overtake Ringo and his men by going in the opposite direction. He kept on. Soon the trail appeared to be no more than five feet wide. The pinto kept going, but was forced to lean so close to the cliff that Fargo's leg brushed the rock face. The horse was both tired and uncertain by this time and frequently pulled up, needing to be pressed on with a touch of Fargo's heels. At one place the path pitched so steeply downward that the pinto's front feet slid along the loose rubble.

Fargo had descended at least a hundred feet when the Ovaro refused to move on. It was pitch-dark by this time. The sky overhead was no help at all. Fargo could not pick out a single star and the moon was hidden by great dark projections of rock that once again loomed ominously over his head.

Fargo peered into the darkness. He thought he could see the dim tracery of the trail extending ahead of him along the cliffside. He applied his spurs gently to the pinto's flanks. But the pony would have none of it. Fargo leaned back in his saddle.

"All right, pony," he muttered. "Which way is it?"

The pony shuddered, shook his head, then gathered its feet close together and began to wind about in small shifts, carefully and slowly, until he had turned himself around completely. Only then, on his way downward once again, did it move on.

Fargo glanced back. In that instant there was just enough light for him to pick out the switchback he had missed in the stygian gloom. Had he insisted on proceeding straight on, he would have launched himself and the pinto into space. He patted the pinto's neck gratefully and told himself that from now on, he would let the pinto lead the way. He had no other choice but to trust the animal. Leaning back in the saddle, he let the reins go slack.

Their progress became much slower from then on. But the pinto moved along steadily. Soon Fargo could hear as well as feel solid ground coming closer. The rocks underfoot were larger. A moment after that discovery, the trail played out through shale and gravel. He pulled up, dismounted, reached down for a rock, and hurled it ahead of him into the darkness. It struck solid ground, the echoes it set off rebounding all around him. He looked up and was able to make out, between two massive peaks, a faint sprinkling of stars.

He took off his hat, wiped his brow with the back of his forearm, slapped his hat back on, and remounted. He was about to continue on when he thought he heard voices far above him. He sat the pinto quietly, listening. But after a considerable wait, he heard nothing more—only the sound of the wind sighing in the few scraggly pines clinging to the slopes around him.

He gave it up and rode on, aware that the walls about him were moving back somewhat. Rounding a bend at that moment, he saw, piled dimly before him, what appeared to be some of the roughest footing he had yet attempted to get through. Dismounting for the second time, he led the pinto around great masses of fallen rock, debris, and fallen pine trees lying breast-high across the trail.

At last he came to an area of bald, weathered rock, the canyon walls fell back, and he could feel the open sky and country looming just beyond him. He glanced up and was rewarded with the sight of a swarm of stars. A moment later a bright orange peel of a moon poked out from behind a peak. He had indeed cut through to White Horn Pass as Compton had told him he would.

By this time exhaustion had almost completely overtaken him, and the feel of the pinto under him communicated the same distress. He came upon a thin stream coursing down the middle of the pass. Dismounting, he filled his canteen and let the pinto have his fill. He was too tired to bother with a campfire. He unsaddled the pinto and rubbed him down despite his weariness, then let him loose to find graze. He slumped down with his back against his saddle and chewed patiently on a sourdough biscuit and a piece of jerky, allowing the tension to melt from his weary frame. Then he pulled his slicker around him and rested his head against the saddle. Before he closed his eyes, he told himself not to sleep beyond the break of day.

Sleep came instantly—like a gentle fist.

Fargo awoke quickly, aware at once of the gray light. Sitting up, he noted the wet tops of the rocks and felt the cold dampness in the air. The outer surface of his slicker was dimpled with faint beads of moisture. He could see his breath in front of him. He got up and stretched, aware of the chill breeze sweeping through the pass. Though this was only September, there was a hint of frost in the high, clear air.

He poked with his rifle barrel along the under edges of the boulders, alert for snakes, then gathered firewood and built his morning campfire. Once he got it going to his satisfaction, he sat his spider pan atop the embers, then placed his last remaining sourdough biscuits into it, melted some bacon fat over them, then dropped in the last of his jerky. The coffee came next, and before long, the aroma of fresh coffee, jerky, and biscuits had effectively chased the early-morning chill.

The pinto had been watching all this attentively, his lips working, his ears snapping forward eagerly. The Ovaro was obviously ready for a change in his grass diet. But as Fargo reached for the pan, the pony raised its head in sudden alarm and took a step backward. At the same instant, Fargo heard the clink of spurs on rock behind him.

Drawing his Colt, he spun around—and found himself peering into the muzzle of Slim's six-gun. His sidekick Sam was right beside him, his own Colt out. Slim's face still bore the marks of his recent brawl with Fargo, and the light in his eyes told Fargo that he was anxious now to even the score.

"Drop the iron, mister," Slim said, "unless you want me to use this."

Fargo hesitated.

Sam said, "You heard Slim, mister. He ain't kiddin'."

Fargo let his Colt drop to the ground. Slim grinned widely, took a quick step forward, and slugged Fargo across the side of the face with the barrel of his revolver. The blow was carefully measured and the tall man put all the force he could muster into it. Fargo felt himself spinning sideways to the ground. The back of his head crunched against a boulder, but he shook off its effects and glared up at the two men.

He felt a mixture of fury and dismay that he had allowed himself to be so easily bushwhacked by these two pieces of shit. But his time would come. He would see to that.

4

"It was Compton told you, wasn't it?" said Slim, leaning close, a sneer on his face.

"Told me what?"

"Where our mine was," Sam spoke up, stepping angrily closer. He seemed anxious to kick Fargo. "We seen ya ride by. You was pretty smart about it. You acted like you didn't even see it. But you looked right at it. We saw you."

"Compton told me nothing about your mine."

"Then, how'd you find that trail?"

"Compton."

"See? You ain't very smart, mister, tryin' to fool us."

"He was just giving me a quick way to get to the pass."

The two men exchanged glances. It was obvious they were trying to decide whether or not to believe him.

"So how come it's so important that you get to this pass?"

"That's my business."

"We can make it ours," Sam exploded, taking a quick step forward.

Slim held his partner back. "They said back there in Big Rock your name's Fargo. Skye Fargo. That right?"

Fargo nodded.

"What are you up to, Fargo?"

"I told you. Whatever it is, it's none of your business."

"Let me get closer," said Sam to Slim. "I'll kick it out of him."

Ignoring Sam, Slim leaned close to Fargo and went swiftly through his pockets. He found the wallet, then the badge Fargo kept folded in it. The moment Slim saw the badge, he looked at it as if he had been stung.

"What the hell! Are you a lawman?"

"Maybe."

"Damn your eyes, mister. What's that supposed to mean?"

Fargo stared icily at the man. "It means get off my back. Both of you."

Slim flung the wallet at Fargo's feet. "You *are* a lawman, then."

Fargo shrugged. He sure as hell didn't feel like an officer of the law; far from it. But he had kept that badge Wolf Caulder had given him—and he *had* been deputized.

Fargo picked up the badge and wallet.

"Who you after?" Slim demanded.

Pocketing the wallet, Fargo just looked at the two men.

"Hell, that ain't no mystery," said Sam, his eyes lighting craftily. "It's Johnny Ringo he's after. That

52

badge says the town of Pierce—and I heard their Wells Fargo office lost a lot of gold dust last week."

"Is it Johnny Ringo?" Slim demanded of Fargo.

Fargo kept his mouth shut, determined to tell these two no more than he had to.

"I got an idea," said Sam, grinning suddenly.

"What?" said Slim.

"Let's take him to Ringo. I'll bet he don't have no idea this lawman's after him. We'll be doing Ringo a big favor, and he ought to pay us good for bringin' this here lawman to him, all hog-tied, wrapped good and proper—like a Christmas present ready to unwrap."

Slim liked the idea. His eyes lit. "Maybe so, Sam. Maybe so. Ringo's still got plenty of gold dust left, and I'm thinkin' he ought to be real generous when we hand this man over to him."

Both men grinned at Fargo and took a step back, their guns still leveled on him. They were going to sell him to Johnny Ringo. Which meant they knew where Ringo was camped. Fargo leaned back against the boulder, troubled but at the same time pleased. He was about to meet Johnny Ringo a lot sooner than he had expected.

Johnny Ringo—or the man Fargo assumed was the gang leader—was squatting by the morning fire, pouring himself a fresh cup of coffee, when Fargo rode into his camp ahead of his two captors. Ringo stood up and flung the coffee away. The others in his camp got to their feet also. Some distance back, standing between two men, Fargo saw a woman and assumed she was Compton's wife.

An annoyed frown on his face, Johnny Ringo watched intently as the three horsemen continued on into his camp. Ringo was tall with a dark olive complexion, blazing dark eyes, and bold eyebrows that canted slightly upward, giving his face a pronounced saturnine cast. For a highwayman on the dodge, he was dressed cleanly and well, with a leather vest and tight-fitting calfskin britches. The sweatband of his black, flat-crowned sombrero was decorated with silver conchos.

With his hands lashed securely behind him, Fargo had some difficulty bringing his pinto to a halt, but he managed. Without a word, he nodded to the gang leader.

Looking past Fargo, Ringo addressed the two men. "Who the hell is this guy? What are you up to, Slim?"

"It's a present for you," Sam told him.

"Speak plain, dammit!"

"This here's a deputy from Pierce, Johnny," Slim explained nervously. "He's trackin' you, for some reason. We figured it might be a good idea to collar him and bring him to you."

"He's a lawman?" Ringo glanced alertly up at Fargo, his dark brows canting devilishly.

"That's right. He's got a badge."

"You from Pierce?" Ringo asked Fargo.

Fargo nodded.

"How's Caulder?"

"That bullet of yours tore up his gut. He's dead."

Ringo's face seemed to cave in. "Oh, Jesus!" he said, wincing. "I must've shot too fast. Hell, I didn't want that bullet to kill him. I aimed for his leg. I just wanted to disable him for a while—not kill him."

"You're a lousy shot, Ringo. Caulder's dead."

Nodding bleakly, Ringo tipped his head slightly and peered reflectively up at Fargo. "What's your name, mister?"

"Skye Fargo."

"Ain't I heard that name before?"

"Maybe."

"And so Skye Fargo's come after me."

Fargo nodded. "With Wolf Caulder's badge."

Ringo studied Fargo's face for a moment longer, then shrugged and stepped back. Addressing Slim and Sam, he said, "Light and set a spell. We still got some hot coffee. You're welcome to help yourself."

"You goin' to take Fargo off our hands, Ringo?"

"I'm thinkin' on it."

Sam had pulled his horse to a halt beside Fargo. He lifted his foot out of his stirrup, placed it against Fargo's side, and pushed. Fargo was flung awkwardly from his saddle, his hands still bound behind him. He struck the ground shoulder first, narrowly missing a large boulder.

Slim roared with laughter at his partner's action. Then he and Sam dismounted quickly. Fargo swallowed the fury that welled up within him as he looked up at the two men. Nudging each other like village idiots, they bent their vacant, foolish faces over him. Sensing his fury, the two men laughed. Then they straightened up and, with yellow grins creasing their swinish faces, began kicking at his unprotected body. They were soon panting from the exertion.

At last, impatient with their behavior, Ringo strode over and pulled both men off Fargo. He was so rough, Sam almost fell to the ground.

"Leave off that, you two," he told them.

"What's the matter?" Slim asked, frowning. "You ain't got a soft spot for this here lawman, have you? Look how far he's come to string you up!"

"That's right," chimed in Sam. "You heard what he told you. He came a long way to see you dancin' at the end of a rope."

"Well, dammit! I didn't send you two buzzards after him," Ringo snapped angrily. "I could have handled him myself easy enough."

"You mean you ain't glad we brung him in for you?" Sam asked.

Johnny Ringo sensed something in Sam's voice. He tipped his head slightly, his eyes narrowing. "All right, let's have it. What the hell are you two vultures after?"

"That ain't very nice, Ringo."

"*Mister* Ringo to you!"

"Come on, Johnny," protested Sam in a voice that was close to a whine. "We just didn't want to see you get shot."

"Bullshit!"

"Well," began Sam with a quick, nervous glance at his partner, "we *was* sort of hopin' you'd see your way clear to splittin' a little of your sudden wealth between us—"

"—'cause we delivered this lawman, trussed up like a turkey, all ready to pluck," Slim finished hopefully. He was obviously more than a little disconcerted at Johnny Ringo's seeming lack of appreciation for their labors on his behalf.

Ringo squinted at the two men as if he had just turned over a stone and found them scurrying away from the light. "Like I already told you," he replied, his voice thick with distaste. "I'll think on it. Now go on over to the fire and get some coffee."

Fargo had managed by this time to push himself to a sitting position, his back against the boulder he had come down beside. His hat was lying in the dust a few feet from him. Ringo picked it up and slapped it down on Fargo's head. Then he unsheathed his bowie and sliced through the rope binding Fargo's wrists.

"I'll send Rose over with some coffee," Ringo told Fargo. "Just sit tight and don't try nothin' foolish." Then he reached over and took Fargo's bowie from its sheath.

Fargo, busy rubbing the circulation back into his wrists, nodded.

Ringo left him and walked over to his gang members and said something to the woman. She left them, filled a cup with coffee, and started toward Fargo. Ringo stayed with his four gang members, evidently discussing with them what to do with Fargo. And possibly the two miners as well.

Rose stopped in front of Fargo and handed him the cup. By this time Fargo was able to use his hands. Thanking her, he reached up and took the coffee from her. She said nothing, just stood over him as he drank.

She was dressed in a man's shirt and Levi's. She filled them out the way no man could. A yellow scarf was knotted at her neck, and her dark hair, thick and curly, hung down to her shoulders. Her face was sharp and her hazel eyes quick. She was not very pretty, but there was a feral look in her smoky eyes and about her loose, sensual mouth that could turn a man on—and keep him on.

Between sips, he said, "Your husband is worried about you."

She was startled. "You know Frank?"

Fargo nodded.

"He sent you after me?"

"He would like it if I could get you away from the gang. He loves you and wants you back."

She laughed. Coldly. Contemptuously. "That fool! I swear, he'd eat my vomit if I told him! Go back to him? I'd rather die!"

"Then you didn't leave against your will?"

"Hell, I would have gone with Murdo if Ringo hadn't killed him. Frank Compton's a loser. I was a fool to have married him. I was better off at Pablo's."

Fargo nodded. He had suspected as much from the very beginning. He handed his empty cup back to Rose and thanked her. She took it from him and spun away, heading back to the campfire.

Watching her go, Fargo wondered at all the men whose women loathed them—and all the women whose husbands were bored silly with them. He had found, as a general rule, that the more a man loved a woman, the more contempt she felt for him—and the more a woman obeyed and remained faithful to her husband, the more unfaithful and restless he became.

It was a trap he would never fall into—if, that is, he ever got out of this one.

Fargo watched as Johnny Ringo left the four men and walked over to the two miners. As he spoke to them quietly, they suddenly erupted in outrage and began protesting loudly. Then Slim went for his side arm. Ringo stepped back. His own Colt cleared leather in a twinkling. Slim's six-gun had not yet left its holster. He let the gun drop back into it as he and Sam backed hastily away from Ringo.

Ringo turned to his men. "Disarm these two." As Ringo's men stepped forward and quickly disarmed Slim and Sam, Johnny Ringo said, "Take their rifles, their knives, everything. Then ride about a half-mile on through the pass and dump them beside the trail. Then keep going. I'll catch up to you."

As the gang members—Rose helping—broke camp, Johnny Ringo walked over to Fargo and hunkered down beside him. Taking out a cheroot, he lit it, then offered one to Fargo. Fargo took it without a word, then leaned close as Johnny Ringo lit it for him.

"That's a nice-lookin' pinto you got there," the outlaw commented.

Fargo inhaled on the cheroot and nodded.

"I'll leave it and the rest of your gear down the road a ways, fully saddled—just in case."

Fargo did not know what Ringo had in mind, but he said nothing and took a deep drag on the cheroot. The four men and the girl mounted up and rode off down the trail, hazing the miners' horses and Fargo's pinto before them as they rode. Fargo watched them go for a while, then went back to his cheroot.

Johnny Ringo stared for a moment at the glowing end of his cheroot, then cleared his throat. "I got to kill you, Fargo. Them two bastards don't leave me no choice in the matter. You know that."

Fargo's craggy face broke into a slight smile. He ran his big hands through his inky-black hair. "I'm real sorry to hear that. But I guess you're right."

"The thing is—I figure I owe you one."

"Why?"

"You was a friend of Wolf Caulder, and he was my friend, too."

Fargo could see that Johnny Ringo was wrestling with a difficult decision. And it all had to do with his memories of his old friend Wolf Caulder, the man he had killed.

"How long ago was it you knew Caulder?" Fargo asked.

"Five, maybe six, years," the outlaw replied, his voice low. He frowned then, peering past Fargo into the distance—remembering. "Caulder found me with a bullet in my gut, near dead by a water hole. I only had a few feet to go, but there was no way in hell I was going to reach that water. Then Caulder rode up. He gave me water, fished the slug out of me. He tended me like a brother till I got back on my feet."

Johnny Ringo went silent then, pulling on the cheroot for a while, his eyes narrow slits as he peered at the coiling smoke.

"Afterward we rode together," he resumed, his

voice still soft. "We pulled a few jobs." He shook his head. "But Wolf didn't like that much. He was always thinking of the poor sons of bitches we was robbin'. He didn't have the heart for it. So he went his way, and I went mine . . . till we met in that express office."

The memory seemed to goad him. He flung away the cheroot and stood up. "Like I said before," he said, smiling bleakly, "I owe you one. For Caulder's sake. So I'm goin' to leave you with those two vermin. I promised them gold if they kill you, but they will have to use their bare hands and bring me that badge of yours as proof. Maybe you can kill them instead. You look big enough. That's the best I can do for you."

Then he turned and strode quickly over to his horse. He said something to the two sullen miners, then stepped into his saddle and spurred off. As the drum of his horse's hooves faded among the rocks, the two miners, licking their lips nervously, started toward Fargo. Slim bent and picked up a fist-sized boulder. Sam did the same. Fargo got to his feet and moved away from the boulder.

Suddenly Sam hurled the rock at Fargo's head, then charged. Fargo ducked aside to avoid the rock. But he was unable to escape Sam's furious rush. The man drove him back against the canyon wall, his head slamming back hard. Lights exploded deep inside his brain. Slim rushed him from the side and brought his rock down hard, aiming for Fargo's head. But Fargo twisted away just in time. The rock glanced harmlessly off Fargo's shoulder. Undaunted, Slim hooked Fargo around the neck with his arm, and with both Sam's weight and Slim's arm pulling on him, Fargo sagged to one knee, still struggling.

He jabbed back with his elbow and managed to break Slim's grip on his neck. At the same time, he lashed out with his left fist and managed to catch Sam under the chin. Sam reeled back, clutching at his Adam's apple. Regaining his feet, Fargo turned his full attention on Slim, battering him with a series of sledging blows to the face and head. As Slim sagged forward, Fargo slammed his knee up into his face. The man's nose exploded.

But by then Sam had recovered. He threw himself on Fargo, pummeling him with an angry flurry of blows that drove Fargo back. His foot caught on something and he went down. Flinging himself upon Fargo, Sam began to pound him about the head and shoulders, Slim joining him.

Fargo covered his face with his forearms, then heaved desperately and managed to roll sideways. Then he hunched up and pushed himself back onto his hands and knees. His right hand found a large rock. He spun about and brought the rock up into Sam's face. The blow crushed the man's cheekbone and sent him flying backward, yelping like a whipped dog. Flailing out wildly then, Fargo managed to throw Slim off him and regain his feet.

As Slim tried to get up also, Fargo kicked him in the face. His boot caught the man in the mouth. Slim reeled backward, spitting out teeth. His heel caught a boulder and he went down heavily on his back—just as Sam, head down, rammed Fargo in the back and drove him forward to the ground. Fargo hit heavily and lay facedown for a second, dazed, then instinctively flung himself over. Sam was standing over him, a huge rock held high over his head.

Fargo rolled swiftly to one side. The rock crunched into the ground beside him, striking him only a glancing blow. Fargo kept on rolling, then scrambled to his feet just in time to meet Sam's next charge. But Sam was near the end of his endurance by this time. He was panting heavily, his breath coming in sharp, painful gasps. Fargo stopped his charge, then drove Sam back with a series of hooking rights and lefts.

When suddenly he caught Sam flush on his nose, Sam howled and staggered back, blood streaming from both nostrils, his eyes filled with tears of pain and rage. Fargo saw a rock. He bent and picked it up. As he did so, Slim grabbed him from behind. He, too, was panting loudly from the exertion. Grappling frantically, the two men thudded heavily to the ground. But Fargo still held the rock. Clubbing it viciously against the side of Slim's head, he saw the man shake himself and try to pull away.

Before he could, Fargo brought the rock down onto the man's skull with all the force he could muster. He felt bone crack. A third time Fargo slammed downward, this blow containing all the fury and pent-up frustration that had built up within him during this near-hopeless fight. Slim's skull shattered and the man fell forward onto the ground, his long body shuddering convulsively.

Exhausted, half-mad with the murderous intensity of the battle, Fargo looked up from the ground to see Sam standing over him with another boulder. Lifting his legs, he hooked one ankle around Sam's feet and pushed with his other foot. Sam lost his balance and fell back, dropping the boulder. The rock just missed Fargo as he roused himself to one final effort and grabbed Sam's right leg as the man tried to crawl away.

Sam thrashed frantically in an effort to pull free of Fargo. Fargo hung on and dragged him to the ground and swung a vicious, sledging blow to the man's chin. Sam's head snapped around from the force of it, his eyes losing their focus. Fargo came back with his left, crawled up onto Sam, and began punching him. In a frenzy, Sam clawed his way out from under Fargo and scrambled to his feet. Leaping to his feet and overtaking him, Fargo grabbed his shirt and spun him around.

A wild blood lust filled Fargo now, banishing his fatigue, filling him with the joy of combat as he punched Sam about the face and head with savage, murderous precision. Sam backed away slowly, unable to do more than paw at Fargo's ruthlessly timed punches. Blood was streaming from his nose and a gash in his cheek, and he began to whimper under Fargo's ceaseless, metronomic blows. Finally—in a desperate, mindless attempt to escape—he put his head down and lunged blindly at Fargo.

Fargo stepped neatly to one side. As Sam hurtled by him, Fargo brought the edge of his palm down on the man's neck. The rabbit punch dropped Sam like a poleaxed steer. Sam hit the ground heavily. He did not move. Fargo looked closer and saw a slowly spreading slick of fresh blood under his face. He went down on one knee and rolled the man over.

Sam had come down on a high, sharply ridged stone embedded firmly in the ground. The blade of the rock had punched a ragged hole between the man's eyes, shattering the bone between the eye sockets and penetrating the brain.

Sam was dead.

Fargo turned him back over on his stomach and got wearily to his feet. For the first time he heard the ugly, rasping sound his breath made as he sucked air into his lungs. The universe spun drunkenly about his head and he was forced to spread his legs like a sailor on a heaving deck to stay on his feet. Though he realized how much he had been battered, he could still feel little, but his knees were out and his shirt was ripped in a dozen places and his fists and sleeves and shirt front were black with blood and dirt.

Steady on his feet at last, he glanced skyward. Two buzzards were drifting lazily overhead like cinders in an updraft. There would be more before long, he realized. He hoped the birds did not get indigestion. Then, still somewhat groggy, he started down the trail. Johnny Ringo had promised he would leave Fargo's pinto and the rest of his gear farther down, and if he did, this would leave Fargo with a sticky situation. He would owe the man he had sworn to apprehend.

A moment later, when he saw his saddled pinto cropping the grass beside the trail, he decided he would worry about what he owed Johnny Ringo later.

5

As soon as Fargo crested the ridge and started along its spine, he pulled his pinto to a halt. He could feel the first faint touches of a wind, chill enough to have come all the way from Canada. He thumbed back his hat to let the wind dry the sweat on his forehead. The day had been a scorcher, considering it was already into October. It was a week after he had left two dead men for the vultures and he was hoping to overtake the Ringo gang in the town ahead.

The trail ran level across the spine of the ridge for about a quarter of a mile before breaking down in a gentle slope to the floor of the valley. From there it disappeared into the well-watered grasslands running north to where the valley ended in a low thrusting of hills. The town of Lawson had been planted alongside a stream just this side of those hills. From where he sat his horse, Fargo could see the glint of the late-afternoon sunlight on the town's windows.

Fargo urged his horse on, eager to reach the town before nightfall. He succeeded. It was still light when he rode into Lawson. As he put his pinto into the hitch rail in front of the Lawson Hotel and dismounted, a huge, bearded individual stepped out of the hotel's saloon. A dusty star was pinned to his buttonless vest.

Fargo knew him. He was Sheriff Pete Barnum. Barnum paused when he saw Fargo dropping his reins over the hitch rail.

"Howdy, Fargo," the man said somewhat warily.

The last time the two had met Fargo had not been particularly sociable. He had been close, he thought, to overtaking one of the two men he was still after and would tolerate no delay. This had caused trouble between Fargo and the sheriff.

But that was years past.

"Howdy, Barnum," Fargo said, mounting the porch steps and thrusting out his big hand.

The sheriff shook it. His grip was still powerful. "What brings you to this country, Fargo?"

"Johnny Ringo."

"You ridin' with his crowd?"

"Not exactly. Is he in town?"

"He is. And he's keeping his tail down and his nose clean."

"Will you be in your office later on?"

"I reckon so."

"I'll see you then."

The sheriff nodded and walked on down the street. Fargo glanced at the not-very-imposing hotel. He hoped to hell it didn't have more gray-backs than beds. He wanted to sleep through this night, for he hadn't entirely shaken off the effects of that struggle with the two miners, and his shoulder was still mighty tender.

He flung his saddlebags over one shoulder,

hefted the rest of his gear onto his other one, and headed into the hotel.

An hour later—bathed, barbered, and well-fed—Fargo went in search of Pete Barnum.

As he had promised, the big man was waiting for him in his office. When Fargo entered, Barnum reached into the bottom drawer of his desk and hauled into view a sorely depleted bottle of brandy and two shot glasses.

Fargo sat down in a wooden chair beside the desk while Barnum poured. They took up their glasses, saluted, and gulped down the contents in one quick dip of their heads.

Barnum grinned as he slapped his empty shot glass down. "Why are you after Johnny Ringo?"

Fargo explained about the express-office raise in Pierce and the death of Wolf Caulder.

"So now you have a badge."

"I guess you might say that."

"Hell, Fargo. It ain't worth a pinch of coon shit, and you know it."

Fargo shrugged.

The sheriff regarded Fargo for a moment, his bushy, beetling brows knitting. His beard was shaded from dark brown to rusty red, and from two narrow slits behind all that hair peered a couple of shrewd, dark eyes, alight now with amusement. "You sure as hell like trouble, Fargo."

"Maybe you know a way to get through this life without trouble?"

"No, I don't—and that's a fact. But some of us seem to go out of our way to get it."

Fargo shrugged and pushed his shot glass toward the sheriff.

As the sheriff filled Fargo's glass and his own, he said, "The thing is, badge or no badge, you have no jurisdiction here. You're in Montana Territory now. And I don't have no information on that raise—and no dodgers on Johnny Ringo. So as far as I'm concerned, Johnny Ringo and his men can come and go as they please, just so long as they keep their noses clean."

"Fair enough."

"And I won't tolerate any gunplay on your part—or Johnny Ringo's."

"You want to keep a nice, quiet town."

"I do. And I want to live long enough to enjoy it. Hell, we'll have schools and churches in this place before long."

"Soon's you convince the Sioux this ain't their land."

"Right," the sheriff said, downing his drink.

Fargo emptied his own glass and stood up. "Guess I'll be getting back to my room," he said. "I'm a tired man."

"You look it."

Fargo met Rose in the hotel lobby. She was no longer wearing a man's shirt and Levi's. But the dress she wore was skimpy, and he could tell she had little on under it. She was startled to see him, but not all that surprised. He did not like the way she looked. Her right cheekbone was bruised and there was a mouse under one eye.

70

"I know," she said bitterly, stopping in front of Fargo. "I don't look so hot."

"No, you don't."

"It ain't Johnny. It's one of his men. Wes."

"I suggest you stay away from him."

She shrugged. "Does Johnny know you're in town?"

Fargo smiled. "He will soon enough. If you don't tell him, I'm sure the sheriff will."

She smiled then. "You're a cool one."

"I am also tired. Good night, Rose."

"If you get lonely, I'll be across the street. In the Drover's Hall. Johnny and Wes are into a high-stakes poker game. It's been going on now since this afternoon. You ought to come over and watch."

Fargo just shook his head wearily and moved on up the stairs to his room. It was already dark, and as soon as he closed the door and locked it, he dragged a chair over to the door, propped it under the doorknob, then walked over to the window and pulled down the shade. Only then did he light the lamp on the dresser and peel out of his buckskins.

Almost as soon as he hit the covers, he slept— only to be awakened by a commotion in the street beneath his window. He got up and looked down. A crowd was milling around in front of the Drover's Hall. He could see men standing on the saloon porch, waving to others to join those already crowding into the saloon. That high-stakes game Rose had mentioned was apparently nearing a climax.

Fully awake by now, Fargo dressed quickly and left the hotel to watch.

*   *   *

Despite the hour—it was close to two in the morning—the saloon was packed, and more were squeezing in. Sheriff Barnum was close by the poker table, keeping a sharp watch on the proceedings. Standing a few steps to one side of Wes was Rose. Her mouth open slightly, she was watching the goings-on with a sweaty, almost lusty intensity.

Fargo looked around for an empty chair, and his size made it simple for him to ease his way through the crowd. Coming to a halt beside Barnum, Fargo nodded a greeting to him, then turned the chair around and straddled it, his eyes on the two players.

Johnny Ringo and two of his gang members had pulled up chairs beside Wes, who was playing the house gambler. Some called the gambler Ace, others Heller. He was a lean, cadaverous man whose eyes peered out from deep hollows. His nose was a blade, and he had a fragile-looking, jutting chin. His hands were long and soft and white. They dealt the cards with a deft expertise that could only have been gained, Fargo mused, after a long apprenticeship on a Mississippi riverboat.

Fargo soon caught the names of the other gang members. Sitting across from Ace Heller was Tex and a fellow they called Coop. Beside Coop sat Johnny Ringo. He had seen Fargo enter and had taken the time to glance in his direction. There was surprise in his eyes. And a query as well. Fargo smiled and nodded politely. Johnny Ringo went back to watching the game.

Judging from the towering stacks of chips in front

of Wes and Ace Heller, there was a great deal of money at stake. It looked to Fargo as if Ringo and his gang, through Wes, were staking their combined worth in gold dust against the house.

"What's goin on?" Fargo asked Barnum softly.

"Wes has been losing his shirt to Heller for a week now," Barnum told him just as softly. "But today, Johnny and the rest of his gang are backing him."

"You didn't tell Johnny Ringo I was in town yet?"

"Didn't have the chance. They been playing this here game since before you rode in."

Fargo nodded and looked back at the game. The two players had discarded and drawn and were now standing pat. The betting began. There were tiny beads of perspiration on Wes' forehead. He looked carefully over at Heller.

"You stayin' in?" he asked.

"Sure am," said Heller, pushing into the pot at least two hundred dollars' worth of chips.

Moistening his lips, Wes pushed out enough to match Heller's bet, then two hundred more. Heller glanced at his hand, shrugged, and pushed out enough chips to meet Wes' bet. Then he raised him two hundred more.

"Table stakes," Wes told Heller. "Remember, we settled on that earlier."

The gambler smiled coldly. "Sure," he said. "Table stakes, it is."

With greedy eyes Wes looked across at Heller's pile of chips, then at his own. Both men had sizable sums in front of them, in the thousands, at least.

"How much you got there?" Wes asked Heller.

73

With a sudden frown, Heller looked down at his chips and counted quickly. Then he looked across at Wes and cleared his throat. "Three thousand, two hundred."

"All of it," Wes said, his voice hoarse. "We bet all of it. That's close enough to what I've got!"

There was a gasp in the room.

Paying no attention to this response, Wes pushed his chips into the pot. As soon as Heller matched him, Wes cried, "I'm calling!"

He slapped his hand down, faceup. Four aces. Every eye turned to Heller. The gambler coolly laid out his hand. Straight flush, king high. Wes was beat. Rose gasped and stepped back. Wes looked at the cards and then at Heller, his face registering an almost maniacal fury.

"You son of a bitch!" he cried. "You cheated." Jumping to his feet, he drew his Colt and aimed it at Heller.

The gambler's right hand appeared to jump as he fired twice up at Wes, using a small .22-caliber derringer he had drawn from his vest pocket. Two neat holes appeared in Wes' vest just over his heart. Wes staggered back, dropping his Colt. Before he crashed to the floor, Johnny Ringo and the others—all slapping leather—jumped back from the table. An instant later, as patrons dived frantically for cover, the saloon reverberated with the thunder of their guns. As their rounds slammed into Heller, the gambler was flung back. His chair tipped over and he fell to the floor.

He was a dead man before he hit it. As he

came to rest, his right arm was flung out, the deringer dropping from his grasp.

"Look!" cried Rose.

The sheriff dropped beside the gambler and pulled what Rose was pointing at out of the gambler's sleeve—a collapsible device holding cards in a metal clip at one end. Fargo recognized it at once. It was a sleeve holdout. Buckled around his bare arm, it had enabled Heller to extend a playing card or cards into his waiting palm whenever he needed them. To activate it, all he had to do was bend his elbow. When the arm was straightened, a rubber band retracted the metal clip that had been holding the card.

The dead gambler and Wes were carried from the saloon. The crowd slowly dispersed. As it did so, Ringo turned to Barnum, "I had a pretty good idea what Heller was using, Sheriff," he said. "But I didn't know about that vest-pocket derringer of his. If Wes hadn't got so riled, he'd be alive now."

"How did you know Heller was using a holdout?" Fargo asked.

Ringo turned to the Trailsman, a slight smile on his dark face. "His cuffs were too wide."

"Dammit!" said the sheriff. "You should've told Wes."

"If I had, Wes wouldn't have been able to make it look so good." As Ringo spoke, he turned to face a bulky, prosperous-looking fellow in a high sombrero who had just pulled to a halt in front of him. A stump of a cigar glowed in his mouth, and there was a grim cast to his florid face.

"I figure we won that pot, Carney," Ringo told the man. "Your house gambler was a cheat."

The big fellow, obviously the saloon's owner, nodded unhappily. "All right," he said, "but you and your boys are no longer welcome in my place. Cash up and get out."

Ringo's swarthy face got noticeably darker, but the sheriff laid a restraining hand on his arm. Ringo settled down, nodded to the other members of his gang, and proceeded to sweep the chips into his hat.

Before Johnny Ringo headed toward the bar to cash them in, he glanced back at Fargo. "You still gunning for me, Fargo?"

"Yes."

"Then I guess I'll be pulling out."

The sheriff and Fargo left the saloon together. As they reached the porch, the sheriff pulled up and looked quizzically at Fargo. "I don't understand it. For two men gunning for each other, you two sure as hell act polite enough."

"It's a long story, Sheriff," Fargo replied. "There are some things about that raise and Johnny Ringo I didn't tell you. And in a way, I owe Johnny Ringo my life."

"And you're still going after him?"

"I can't back off now."

Barnum shook his head. "It sure sounds crazy to me."

"You ever known anything to be as simple as it looks? Take a woman, for example."

The sheriff chuckled and shook his head. "I guess

maybe you're right at that. But I don't want any more gunplay in this town. Not tonight, I don't."

"I won't start it, Barnum, if there is any—and that's a promise."

"That's good enough for me, Fargo."

The two men parted and Fargo walked across the street to the hotel.

When he entered his dark hotel room a moment later, he reached over for the chair and again jammed it up against the doorknob. As he turned then to see to the window shade, he caught a movement in the shadows by it. Instantly he ducked to one side, his Colt materializing in his right hand.

"Don't shoot!" Rose cried. "It's me!"

"What the hell?"

"I had to see you!"

Fargo closed the door, holstered his weapon, then lit the lamp on the dresser. Rose slumped into the ragged, upholstered rocker beside Fargo's bed, her hands clasped forlornly in her lap.

"What do you want?" Fargo asked warily.

"They killed Wes."

"You mean Ace Heller did."

"Johnny Ringo rigged it so Wes would die. I swear it, Fargo."

Fargo looked at her for a long moment, then shrugged. "I suppose it is likely. What do you want me to do about it?"

"Take him. Take him now, while you can."

"You don't like him. Is that it?"

"He's abandoning me here," she snapped. "He says he doesn't want me with him any longer."

"That's his choice to make, isn't it?"

"But Wes said I could stay."

"I thought Wes was the one who beat you up."

"He . . . he was just a little drunk, is all. He made it up to me."

"Well, there's nothing I can do, Rose. And maybe it's a good thing. This way, with you out of it, you won't get caught in any cross fire."

She got up quickly and walked over to him. Looking up at him, she smiled. "Please. Let me stay here with you tonight."

Her meaning was obvious. "No," he said.

"Why? Are you afraid of me?" she challenged. "Don't you think you're man enough for me?"

"It ain't that," he said. He didn't want to tell her why he didn't want her that night. He did not wish to be unkind.

"I don't trust Johnny," she told him. "It won't be safe for me to go back to my room."

He didn't believe her. But how could he tell her that? And suppose she *was* telling the truth?

"You can stay," he told her wearily.

Chuckling with delight, she unbuckled his gun belt and pushed him down onto the bed. Lying on his back on the bed, he watched her peel out of her clothes. He had been right earlier. She was wearing practically nothing under her dress. Then she stripped him, pushed him farther up on the bed, her hot fingers coaxing him to an erection. She didn't have to work very hard. With a squeal of delight, she frenched him, then snuggled down beside him, purring, not like a kitten, but like a wildcat.

78

Then she climbed on top of him. "Yes," she told him fiercely. "Me on top! I want to ride you like you ride that pretty pinto. And I will be slow, Fargo. So slow it will drive you mad."

"Try me," he said.

Suiting action to words, she suspended herself astride him and then lowered herself onto his erection. She did it with a hearty recklessness that caused his heart to skip a beat, then wriggled her behind just a little and settled still more onto him, so that he was completely enveloped by the moist, enclosing warmth of her. She began to rock then, slowly, as she had promised. Only imperceptibly did she increase the pace of her rocking motion.

She was an expert, no doubt of that.

She looked down at him as if from a great height, smiling happily, tiny beads of perspiration standing out on her face, her tongue running back and forth along her partly opened mouth. Giving him pleasure was delighting her as much as it did him. Her tempo increased. And then she flung her head back and closed her eyes. He saw her face harden into a grimace of pleasure.

By that time Fargo was lost in the expert frenzy of this woman. She was riding him now, not wildly, but caressingly and with infinite skill. Each downward thrust of her body seemed to meld them into one complete, passionate entity. Each time she rose along his shaft, he felt a momentary terror that she would lose him. But each time she stopped just in time and was plunging down upon him again, and he was thrusting mightily up to meet her.

Her climax came almost before he was aware of

it. He heard her gasping shriek, and then she was leaning forward, her breasts slamming into his chest, her fists beating him about the shoulders. He grabbed her wrists and held her, then flung both of his arms around her and rose into her again and again, astonished at the repeated orgasms exploding from his groin.

And then she was rolling off him, her lips covering his face, his chest, his arms, then his stomach. He wanted to tell her that she had wrung the last ounce from him, but he never got the words out as her mouth enclosed his near-flaccid erection. Her tongue worked furiously, expertly. It became a flame igniting him, and before long he was not only erect, but reaching out savagely for her, pulling her up onto him and then swinging over onto her, intent now on taking her the way she had taken him.

"Yes!" she hissed as he plunged deep within her.

She fastened her lips to his. Their tongues embraced. Fargo was only dimly aware of Rose beneath him as he pounded away. Both of them were swept up in the frenzy of their coupling. At times he was afraid he might be hurting her, and would begin to ease up. Then her fierce cries of outrage would come as she tightened her legs about his waist and flung herself recklessly up against him. He found himself laughing, finally, and at the end of it, nearing the peak, he flung back his head and almost howled . . .

As he rolled off Rose a moment later, his hands tangled in her dark curls, she smiled at him, then ran her tongue over her lips.

"Mmmm," she said. "That was nice."

Fargo nodded. He wanted to sleep now. It had been a long, long day and that short nap he had had before going back downstairs was not sufficient. "You can stay with me for the night, Rose," he told her.

"For the night? Is that all?"

"Yes."

For a moment her hazel eyes went cold. Then they softened. "We'll see," she said, reaching out and holding her hand against his cheek. "We'll see about that."

Fargo shrugged, got up, and took his Colt from his gun belt. Returning to the bed, he tucked it under his pillow, his right hand about the grips. She watched him warily.

"Just a precaution," he told her.

She nodded and pulled the covers up over her. As she rolled over, he turned off the lamp and closed his eyes. He was almost asleep when he caught the pause in Rose's steady breathing. He thought he heard light footsteps in the hallway outside his door. He feigned sleep and waited. After a long moment, Rose eased herself out from under her covers on her side of the bed and stole across the room to the door. He heard her carefully move the chair to one side. Her hand touched the doorknob. As the door swung open, Fargo rolled off the bed.

"He's got a gun," Rose cried to the three men who rushed into the room past her.

But her warning came too late. Fargo was already firing from the floor under the bed. He caught the first intruder low. The man crumpled up and toppled to the floor. The other two pulled up, confused, and began firing blindly at the bed. The terrific detonations filled the room. Fargo's next round sent another one reeling back out through the open door. Someone out of sight in the hallway began blasting in at the bed. Fargo fired back. Rose cried out.

Then Fargo cleared the doorway with a steady fusilade from his Colt.

6

As nightshirted roomers appeared outside the door, Fargo got to his feet and lit the lamp. By that time the night clerk had pushed his way into the room, only to come to a dismayed halt just inside the door as he looked down at the two men twitching on the floor.

"How's the girl?" Fargo asked.

The clerk looked at him and swallowed. "I . . . don't know," he managed.

The sheriff pushed his way into the room. He had heard Fargo's question. "Rose's got a broken arm, looks like," he told Fargo. "And it's a bloody mess right now."

"But she'll be all right?"

"Sure. The doc's looking after her. You want to tell me what happened here?"

"What's it look like to you?"

"A goddamned Mexican revolution."

"You recognize them?"

"Sure. They're Johnny Ringo's men."

"Rose let them in."

Barnum glanced shrewdly at Fargo. "Was she worth taking that much of a chance?"

Fargo shrugged. "She was good enough."

One of the men on the floor alongside the door stirred, then groaned. Both men turned to look at him. This was the one they called Tex. He was lying on his back, his mouth open, the left side of his shirt dark with blood, his six-gun still clutched loosely in his hand. The other one, Coop, was lying crumpled, facedown, just in front of the bed. It looked as if someone had dug a hole in his back with a pickax.

Fargo glanced over at the stunned roomers still crowding the doorway. "Get the hell out of here," he told them.

They pulled hastily back.

The sheriff followed after them and shut the door in their faces, then turned to Fargo. "I didn't see Johnny when I came up here. He might still be in the hotel. You think he'll come after you?"

"No. Not now."

At that moment they heard a horse clattering down the street. Fargo went to the window and looked down. A lone rider had just burst out of the livery stable across the street and was heading out of town. From the look of the horse and the set to the man's shoulders, it appeared to be Johnny Ringo.

Beside Fargo, Barnum commented, "He must think your luck is too good. And maybe he's right."

"It ain't my luck. It's his. And it's been pretty good so far."

"What do you mean?"

"With my help and the help of that fool gambler, Johnny now has all that gold dust to himself."

"You think he planned it that way?"

"Don't matter if he did or not. That's the way it turned out."

There was a sharp rap on his door. The desk clerk and the hotel owner rushed in, the doctor on their heels.

"Self-defense," the sheriff told the hotel owner as the doctor set his bag down beside Tex. "Johnny Ringo and his boys tried to cut down your guest."

"And I'd like another room," Fargo told him.

The hotel owner was appalled at what he found. He mopped his brow with a handkerchief and looked, wide-eyed, at Fargo. "Of course," he said.

Fargo dressed, gathered up his gear, and left the room, the clerk leading him down the hall to another room. By that time one of the dead men was being carried from his room while the doctor tended to the other one. For no reason other than that bullheaded stubbornness, the fellow with the hole in his back was still alive.

The sheriff went with Fargo to his door. "You think you'll be able to sleep after this?"

As the clerk fled back down the hallway, Fargo paused in the open doorway and looked back at Barnum. "Sure. Why?"

"I just wondered."

"Any other reason?"

"Yeah. I want you to get a good night's sleep so you can ride out of here fresh as a daisy first thing in the morning."

"You want to get rid of me?"

"Trouble follows you, Fargo, I been noticing."

"Suits me, Barnum," Fargo said, stepping into his room. "I got a man to catch."

He closed the door.

As Fargo rode out early the next morning, he saw Rose watching him from her hotel window, her left arm in a sling. As soon as he glanced up at her, she ducked back out of sight. Fargo was glad she was well enough to be up and about. He didn't want her to suffer any more than was necessary. After all, she had spiked her betrayal of him with a bit of spice. A woman with her talent would surely not languish unappreciated in this town for long.

Johnny Ringo's tracks led west, toward the distant Sawtooths. Fargo pushed his pinto to the limit. The powerful Ovaro responded magnificently, and before nightfall, Fargo saw a horseman he was certain was Johnny Ringo cresting a ridge a few miles ahead of him.

Fargo pressed on until nightfall, then made a dry camp.

By noon the next day, he was within a half mile of Johnny Ringo. Then he topped a rise. A long flat lay before him. It was empty. Fargo pulled the pinto to a halt and examined the flat closely. Nothing marred its undulating pelt of grass. Steep, pine-clad flanks crowded it on both sides. And less than twenty miles in the distance, the great shouldering foothills hunkered like sentinels before the towering peaks beyond, which were already capped with snow.

Fargo put the pinto down the slope to the flat, his eyes searching the grass for sign. He found none.

Returning to the ridge he had left, he began moving in an easterly direction along it, just below its crest. Again he found no sign. Doubling back, he went west this time, still keeping below the crest of the ridge. A few hundred yards before he reached the pine slope ahead of him, he saw hoofprints. He dismounted and examined them. They were from Johnny Ringo's horse. A nail on the left front shoe on Ringo's black left a telltale dimple. Mounting up, he followed the tracks into the timber. Before long, Johnny's sign petered out on the slick pine needles carpeting the ground.

Four days later, deep in the mountains, Fargo dismounted beside a stream. It was noon and time for a break. He watered the pinto, filled his canteen, and sat with his back to a tree as he let his thoughts continue along a track they had been exploring for the past couple of days.

Up until now Ringo had successfully used Fargo and others to separate himself from his gang members. This gave him most of the loot from the express-office raise. He had dealt with Murdo himself, but it was Fargo who took care of those two troublesome miners. The gambler had been maneuvered into killing Wes, and Rose—along with Fargo—had been instrumental in taking care of the rest, and if Ringo had been just a mite luckier, he would have been able to get rid of Fargo at the same time.

But now it was just between the two of them.

Fargo was almost certain that Johnny Ringo had a place somewhere in these mountains, that this was the land he fled to after a raise, when he wanted to put behind him the life he lived outside these mountains. With that in mind, Fargo saw his best hope was to keep moving and probing and do little to hide his presence. He would find Ringo eventually—or Ringo would find him. It really didn't matter which, since it would amount to the same thing in the end.

This much settled in his mind, Fargo stirred to life and began to gather kindling for a campfire. He wanted fresh coffee.

Not long after, his stomach filled with jerky and sourdough biscuits washed down with the coffee, Fargo leaned back against a pine and slowly, carefully withdrew his Colt from its holster. Pretending to be asleep, he rested his head back against the tree, cradling the big Colt out of sight in his lap. For the past few seconds—though he couldn't be absolutely certain—Fargo thought he heard someone pulling himself across the pine needles toward him.

Fargo waited until the last possible moment, then rolled away from the tree and jumped up. A huge half-breed, dressed in torn Levi's and a ragged cotton shirt, left the ground in a swift leap. A long blade flashed in his right hand. Fargo parried the knife thrust with his Colt as the force of the half-breed's charge drove him backward down the slope. His heel struck a root and he went down heavily, the half-breed atop him.

Twice the half-breed's blade slashed down, but each time Fargo was able to parry the blow. As he struggled, he found the man's dark, gleaming eyes inches from his own. After a fierce, punishing struggle, Fargo managed to clip the half-breed on the side of his head with the barrel of his Colt. It was a powerful, well-timed blow. With a grunt, the half-breed rolled off Fargo, the knife dropping from his fingers.

Fargo kept after him, clubbing him again. The man collapsed facedown onto the ground. Fargo rolled him over and dropped astride him, his knees pinning the man's arms. The half-breed's eyes flickered open. Fargo smiled and rested the muzzle of his six-gun against his windpipe. The half-breed closed his eyes and waited.

Only then did Fargo become aware of the man's condition. Someone had blasted a piece out of his side. His Levi's, all the way down to his knees, were a gleaming shield of blood. The half-breed lay still beneath Fargo, his chest only barely rising and falling as he waited stoically for Fargo's bullet to crash through his windpipe.

Slowly, carefully, Fargo pulled the muzzle away from the man's throat.

The half-breed's dark eyes flashed open. His face hardened. "Kill me!" he hissed. "You white bastard!"

"No."

"Then give me your horse."

"No."

The half-breed lashed out at Fargo. Fargo quieted him with a not-too-gentle rap on the head. The half-breed fell back.

"The Clampetts," he hissed. "They're after me."

"Why?"

"They take my woman. When I take her back, they try to kill me."

Fargo heard the soft pound of hooves above him in the timber. "Is that them?"

"Yes!"

Fargo had no idea who these Clampetts were. But if this man was telling the truth, he would like to stop them, if he could. "You want to take these hombres?"

The half-breed frowned. "You and me? We take them?"

"Why not?"

The man nodded emphatically, a terrible smile lighting his dark face. Fargo dug in the pine needles for the half-breed's knife and handed it to him. Then he thrust the muzzle of his six-gun into the man's stomach.

"Roll over on top of me," Fargo instructed. "Hold the knife to my throat. Don't try anything, or I'll blow a hole in you. Wait until I give the signal before turning on the Clampetts. You got all that?"

"Yes."

Fargo let the half-breed crawl up onto his body, his face leaning close to Fargo's, the blade of his knife held tightly against the skin under his chin. Gently, Fargo eased the muzzle of his six-gun farther into the breed's stomach and thumb-cocked. the half-breed pulled back slightly, his blade no longer pressing so tightly against Fargo's neck.

Turning his head slightly, Fargo glimpsed the two riders dismounting rapidly, then breaking through the pines, guns drawn. Both were thin and wiry, with gaunt faces and high cheekbones. Their clothes hung loosely on their skeletal frames. Each had a wild gleam in his eyes.

"Pull back, Charlie," the nearest one cried, marching to within a few feet of them, his six-gun trained on the half-breed. "We got you dead to rights now!"

Charlie just turned his head and stared blackly up at the Clampetts.

"Stand back, Will," cried the other one. "Let me get a clear shot at the son of a bitch!"

"Now hold your hosses, Jody," Will protested, glancing back over his shoulder. "We got a witness! You willin' to kill them both?"

Jody grinned. "That depends."

Will looked back at his brother. "On what?"

Before Jody could respond, Fargo nudged Charlie. With a sudden bound, the man flung himself on Will and began slashing. Will broke back, his gun falling to the ground. Fargo rolled all the way over and fired up at Jody. His slug caught Jody in the forearm. With a cry the man let loose his gun and staggered back, clutching at his gouting wound. Glancing over at the half-breed, Fargo saw that he had already subdued Will, who was flat on his back with the half-breed on top. Will's shirt was sliced open and there was a superficial wound running down his front. At the moment, the blade of Charlie's knife was digging cruelly into his prominent Adam's apple.

Still covering Jody, Fargo scrambled to his feet and saw that Charlie's knife was drawing blood. He reached down and pulled the half-breed off Will. Then he handed Will's six-gun to Charlie, picked up Jody's revolver, and stuck it into his belt. Then he walked over to the wounded man. Jody was leaning back against a tree, holding to his shattered forearm, his face as white as a sheet.

"You dirty son of a bitch," Jody panted angrily. "You was in cahoots with this breed all the time!"

Fargo slapped Jody so hard his head almost left his shoulders. Forgetting his mangled arm, Jody clutched the side of his face.

"Next time you call me a son of a bitch, you better be ready to eat crow," Fargo told him.

"Now you listen here," Jody cried, his voice almost a wail. "You watch out or my pa'll come after you!"

"He should've come after *you*," Fargo remarked, "a good long time ago."

Fargo turned to Will, the older of the brothers. He was nervously rubbing his throat where Charlie's knife had sliced through the skin.

"Maybe you'd better explain what's going on here," Fargo drawled.

"Go eat shit. I ain't explainin' nothin' to you!"

"I explain," said Charlie.

"Go ahead."

"These two take my woman. Then they steal my horse and come after me. They want to kill me and bury me, so it look like I go away, leave my woman. But when they shoot me, I run off. I need your horse so I can escape. That is why I come at you."

"You should have asked."

"How did I know you would help?" Charlie looked at Will. "I will tell your father what you do. He will fix you. He is man of God."

"Pa won't listen to no breed."

Charlie looked back at Fargo. "We take these two back to John Clampett's place. Clampett, he will punish them good. And he will make them give back my woman and my horse."

"You sure you can trust him?"

"He is a minister of the gospel. He reads the Bible over the dead and make many marriages."

Fargo shrugged. The fact that a man was a Bible-thumper carried little weight with him, but then this half-breed had to know Clampett better than he did.

It was close to dusk when the Clampett ranch came into view. Fargo was astride his pinto, Charlie was riding Will's horse, and leading Jody's. The half-breed had bound up his wound. It was no longer bleeding, and he sat Will's horse without too much discomfort. The brothers were stumbling along just ahead of them, a sullen Will in the lead, a whining Jody right behind him.

The Clampett ranch was a big, sprawling outfit, its buildings spread in among cottonwood and pine. The main ranch house was a log affair, consisting of one long room and a wing built on the south end, which served as the bunkhouse. A cluster of sheds and corrals were scattered about the compound. They were well up into the foothills by this time, and the slopes lifting away from the ranch were thick with ponderosa pine and heavy timber.

As soon as they broke into the clear, Will and Jody cried out to the house. A moment later a big man, rifle in hand, emerged and paused on the low veranda. He shaded his eyes to look more closely, then stepped off the porch and started toward them. Three ranch hands boiled out of the bunkhouse and chased after their boss. They, too, were carrying rifles.

Stumbling, Jody turned his head to glare up at Fargo and Charlie. "You two is going to get your asses whupped now!"

Will said nothing. He just stopped walking and sank wearily to the ground.

Fargo pulled up his pinto. Charlie halted also. In a moment Fargo and the half-breed were surrounded by four gun-toting men. As Jody and Will stumbled off toward the ranch house, two women burst from the house to meet them. One of them began winding a bandage around Jody's shattered arm. The elder Clampett, his face grim, his eyes blazing, glared up at Fargo and Charlie, his rifle leveled on them.

"Them two no-accounts belong to you?" Fargo inquired casually.

"Them's my boys, if that's what you mean," the man responded angrily.

"They stole my woman and took her up to your line shack, Mr. Clampett," Charlie told him. "When I brought her back to my place, they tried to kill me."

"That so?" Clampett observed calmly. He took a step back and covered both of them with his rifle. "Get off them horses real slow like."

Fargo glanced at Charlie. "I thought you said he was a God-fearing man?"

Charlie looked bleakly at Fargo and shrugged.

Fargo dismounted, then Charlie. Fargo turned to face John Clampett. The rancher was studying them both coldly. As tall as Fargo, Clampett was thin enough to take a bath in a rifle barrel, his height accentuated by his lack of heft. There appeared to be not an extra scrap of tallow on his long, bladelike bones. His wrists were long and slender, as were his fingers. Like his two son's, his Adam's apple was prominent. His intricately wrinkled face had been tanned almost black by the sun. His eyes, peering out of deep hollows, were dark blue, almost black. But it was not their color that impressed Fargo, it was their hypnotic intensity.

They were the eyes of a fanatic.

"What about this man's woman?" Fargo asked, indicating Charlie with a nod of his head. "Are your boys in the habit of using a woman in this fashion?"

"Marylou's a white woman who consorted with a half-breed!"

"What the hell difference does that make?" Fargo replied.

"If you don't know, you're as benighted as Charlie here."

The three ranch hands standing behind Clampett snickered, their yellow teeth gleaming like fangs.

"You mean a half-breed ain't fit to sleep with a white woman," Fargo said.

"Not while there's decent white men handy."

"You mind tellin' me where in the Bible it says that?"

"Hell, I ain't havin' no religious disputation with a drifter and a half-breed who just shot up one of my boys. Besides, even if it don't say that in the Bible, it damn well ought to!"

"I suggest you put that rifle down, Clampett—and show a stranger proper hospitality."

Clampett turned to the three hands, a cold merriment lighting his gaunt features. "You hear that, boys? All right! Let's show them Clampett hospitality."

The three men laughed.

"Where'll we put them?" one man asked.

"That feed room in the back of the horse barn. There's plenty of feed in there to keep their guts full."

This really amused the ranch hands.

"Pete," Clampett said, "get a chair and keep guard outside the door after you truss them up. I don't want them gettin' loose." He glanced up at the sky. "There's going to be a full moon tonight—and that means a good night for huntin'."

The one called Pete nodded eagerly, his wolfish face breaking into a grin. He knew what Clampett meant, evidently, and he appeared to be pleased at the prospect.

Fargo offered no resistance as he and Charlie were disarmed and led off to the feed room. But his mind was racing. At this rate, he would never find Johnny Ringo—or anyone else. He had fallen into the hands of a certified, 100 percent nut.

7

The ranch hand that trussed them up did not do a very thorough job. As soon as he locked them in the room and took his post outside the door, the two men promptly maneuvered around so that Fargo could undo Charlie's wrists, who in turn untied Fargo. As soon as they were free, they approached the flimsy door and took turns looking out through a crack.

Fargo saw the back of their guard's head as he sat beside the door, his Henry repeater rifle resting stock down on the floor between his knees. The two men conferred softly. They would break through the door and disarm the ranch hand. It should not be too difficult, both agreed.

They moved back from the door. Fargo was the biggest, so he was the one assigned the task of bursting through the flimsy door. Charlie would follow and overpower the guard.

"Ready?" Fargo asked Charlie.

Charlie nodded.

At that moment they heard the chair's front legs come down and the sound of the man's boots striking the wooden floor. Immediately, two quick shots from his six-gun sent slugs through the door. It was a miracle neither Fargo nor Charlie was hit. Both men flung themselves to the floor.

"Hey, you two in there," the guard called. "Keep still, dammit. Next time I hear you moving about I'll turn this door into a sieve."

Fargo turned his head and looked at Charlie. "I think he means it."

Charlie nodded.

Slowly, carefully, the two men scrunched up to the wall beside the door. They would obviously have to devise another plan, and while they were trying to do this, Fargo and Charlie White Horse introduced themselves formally. Charlie's father, Fargo learned, had been a full-blooded Crow, his mother a Methodist missionary who died when he was a baby. He learned also that John Clampett and his clan were not ranchers. They were moonshiners.

Night fell, and still they hadn't decided what to do. Each time they moved, the fellow sent a shot through the flimsy wall. One round came so close to Fargo's head he thought he could feel its passage.

"What did Clampett mean about the hunting?"

"I think I know," said Charlie.

"I'm listening."

"Some in town say Clampett and his boys like to punish them they find trespassin' on their land by setting the dogs on them, and then hunting them down through the hills. I think maybe that is what he mean."

"He has dogs?"

"Yes. Three hounds. He keeps them in a kennel in back of the main house. They are good trackers."

"We better get the hell out of here."

"Sure. But how?"

Fargo shrugged. "Maybe when they change guards. This one here's a maniac."

"Maybe they don't change guards."

Fargo did not like to think about that. He changed the subject. "This town you mentioned. How far away is it and what's it called?"

"Clay Springs. It's ten miles from here, over the pass."

"I'm lookin' for an hombre calls himself Johnny Ringo. He might be set up in that town. Ever here tell of him?"

"No."

Fargo nodded. He wasn't surprised. Ringo would probably be using an alias anyway. Fargo had never heard of Clay Springs before this, and there was a good chance he'd pick up Ringo's trail there. But first things first. What he had to do now was get away from Clampett and make it to Clay Springs.

The sudden baying of dogs filled the night.

"Here they come," said Charlie.

Fargo whispered, "If we're going to make our move, we better do it now."

Suddenly Fargo heard a moaning cry from outside the door and the sound of the guard's chair overturning.

"Now!" Fargo said. He jumped up, put his shoulder down, and rammed the door. It splintered, but held. Charlie rammed into it right beside him and the door gave way. As Fargo stumbled out of the room, he saw in the dimness a slim, dark-haired woman standing over the guard, a six-gun held like a club in her hand.

"Marylou!" Charlie cried.

She flung herself into his arms. "I didn't know what to do," she cried. "Will came for me and brought me here. I heard them talking. They're going to hunt you down and kill you! Hurry!"

"Where'd you get the gun?" Fargo asked her.

"From Will. I . . . I think I killed him." She was feverish with excitement, a willowy, full-bosomed woman with fine eyes and a strong chin. It was easy to see why men would covet her—Will and Jody, especially.

Fargo snatched up the Henry rifle from the unconscious guard and searched through his pockets for shells. Charlie grabbed the man's Colt and strapped on his gun belt. Fargo wanted to go back into the barn for his pinto and the rest of his gear, but the baying of the hounds and the cries of the men urging them on was coming rapidly closer.

They would have to make for the timber—now.

"Let's go!" said Fargo.

Once in the timber they split. Charlie White Horse and Marylou branched off to the north while Fargo kept on westward toward the pass. Soon thereafter, Fargo heard the hounds break into two packs. Two dogs moved west after Charlie and Marylou, and the other dog began to gain inexorably upon Fargo.

An hour or so later, Fargo glimpsed a moonlit ridge ahead of him on the far side of a broad flat.

Immediately he cut across the flat and clambered up into the rocks fronting the ridge—and waited.

He didn't have long to wait.

The dog, still on a leash, its tail wagging excitedly, its muzzle to the ground, broke onto the flat, its three handlers moving after it. Fargo could not make out the faces of the men. But one of them, the tallest, he was sure was John Clampett himself. As the men got closer, Fargo heard Clampett's voice telling the men to let the dog loose.

Clampett was not dumb. He had seen at once what Fargo's sudden dash across the flat to the ridge indicated.

The dog was set loose. Joyously, baying now in full cry, it raced across the moonlit flat, heading straight for Fargo's position in the rocks. Fargo levered a fresh cartridge into the Henry's firing chamber. He wished he had had his Sharps. This Henry did not have the Sharps' reach. So he waited.

He began tracking the dog when it got to within at least twenty yards of the rocks. For a moment he felt a deep reluctance to pull the trigger. This hound bounding toward him was a fine animal, doing only what it had been trained to do. It was not his fault that its master had put it to such a hellish project. Fargo took a deep breath, sighted on the dog's chest, and squeezed off a shot.

The dog yelped and rolled over, dead on the instant.

Fargo heard an instant cry of dismay erupt from the men as they scattered swiftly. But even as they did so, they sent a rapid fire at the spot in the rocks from which Fargo's gunflash had come. Fargo kept his head down as the rocks around him came alive with ricocheting slugs, tracked the nearest Clampett hand, and squeezed off another shot. The man stumbled once, then fell. Clampett turned then with the others to race back across the moonlit flat. Fargo stood up, sighted carefully, and sent a round after Clampett. He thought he saw the man stagger a moment before he disappeared into a dim confusion of boulders on the far edge of the flat.

Fargo waited a moment or so longer. Without their hound, they had no recourse but to go back to the ranch. The night's hunt was over. Fargo moved farther up into the rocks and kept going until he gained the crest of the ridge. Then, keeping low, he turned west.

He could still hear the other two hounds in the distance. If he was in time, he might be able to give Charlie White Horse and Marylou some assistance.

Fortunately, the hounds chasing Charlie and Marylou were noisy. By cutting always toward their barking, Fargo soon found himself emerging from a stand of timber on a steep slope where, below him, Charlie and Marylou were plunging across a shallow stream. Fargo was some distance behind them, but the moonlight was so bright Fargo could see clearly the pursuing hounds and their three handlers breaking from the timber.

As Charlie and Marylou waded across the stream and clambered up onto the opposite bank, one of their pursuers got off a shot. Fargo saw Charlie fall, then pull Marylou down beside him, after which they crawled toward a dark smudge of rocks above the embankment. A second later, as the men and their hounds swept toward the stream, Charlie returned their fire with his Colt.

At that distance it was at best a futile shot, but it was enough for his pursuers. They released the dogs and sent them baying into the stream.

Charlie White Horse was game. He held his fire, waiting until the first dog gained the opposite bank. Then he fired. The dog spun about, yelping, and plunged back into the water. Undaunted, the second dog piled up onto the bank and started for Charlie and Marylou. Charlie fired again. The hound flopped over and then, whining piteously, began to drag itself around and back to the water.

At once, Fargo slanted swiftly down through the timber, levering a fresh cartridge into the Henry's firing chamber as he did so. Not fifty yards behind the three men, he opened up on them. They were already confused and disheartened by the loss of their hounds. Fargo's fire caused them to scatter in dismay. One of them crashed to the ground—and if Fargo was not mistaken, his arm had been in a sling.

Jody Clampett, he realized as he kept after the other two.

But they had already disappeared into the timber. Fargo saw no sense in going in after them. He returned to Jody, intending to do what he could to help him. But as he approached the downed man, Jody threw up his six-gun and got off two quick shots. The rounds came close and Fargo flung himself flat on the ground. Levering rapidly, he emptied the Henry into Jody.

At last he got warily to his feet and approached the bloody hulk lying facedown in the grass, all that was left of Jody Clampett.

Flinging the empty Henry aside, he turned away and waded across the stream to where Charlie White Horse and Marylou were waiting for him.

"I hear your shots, and I wonder," Charlie said, grinning.

"You hurt bad?"

"It is nothing."

"Where you hit?"

"In my shoulder. It is not deep. The bullet go through it. I do not even lose much blood."

"I'll take care of him," Marylou told Fargo.

Fargo nodded.

"We have cabin in mountains," Charlie White Horse told him. "The Clampetts will not find us. We share it with Crooked Elk. Come with us, Fargo."

"I am going back for my pinto and the rest of my gear."

"I go with you, then."

"No. You're hurt. I'll go alone. Where's this cabin of yours?"

"Follow this stream to rapids, then look for white blaze of rock to your right and ridge of pines. The cabin is beyond ridge, high on the slopes. It is well hidden."

Fargo nodded. But he did not think he would need to bother them or this Crooked Elk fellow. After he dealt with Clampett, he was anxious to get on to Clay Springs and seek out Johnny Ringo. Hopefully, this business with the Clampetts would flush out the gunman. This badge had a strange, uncanny hold over him now, it seemed—almost as if it, not he, were in control.

"Thanks," he said to Charlie White Horse and Marylou. "Maybe I'll see you two again. If not, goodbye and good luck."

"Good luck to you, too, Fargo," Charlie replied.

Fargo turned and started back.

A wailing was coming from the Clampett's ranchhouse. And well it might, Fargo mused grimly, as he stepped cautiously into the horse barn. He found his Ovaro in an unclean, narrow stall in the rear.

Just as he had feared, no one had even bothered to unsaddle the animal. Though Clampett had taken his Colt and gun belt, the Sharps still remained in its scabbard. He checked through the saddlebags and saddle roll. Nothing was missing.

Carefully, his hand held gently over the pinto's nose, Fargo led the pony out through the back of the barn and into the timber beyond. He kept going for a full quarter of a mile before tethering the pony. He knew the horse needed grain and water, but that would have to wait.

He returned to the Clampett's ranch. The lamps were on inside the ranchhouse and the bunkhouse. Men were coming and going between the two buildings. Fargo slipped across the compound and glanced in one of the ranchhouse windows.

Clampett was at the kitchen table, his shoulder being bandaged by a woman who was likely his wife. Three unhappy hands, including the worthy who had been guarding Fargo and Charlie White Horse, were standing to one side. Hovering anxiously alongside his father, a distraught Will was trying to convince Clampett that they would have to wait until daylight to go back after Jody.

Clampett was adamant, however. He was insisting that as soon as he was able to mount up again, he would be leading them all back to find Jody.

Fargo cut back through the darkness toward two smaller barn-like structures huddled together alongside the horse barn. Earlier, Fargo had assumed these buildings sheltered chickens or other small livestock. But if Charlie White Horse was correct, it would be inside one of these structures that Fargo would find the stills Clampett used to brew his moonshine.

Reaching the first building, he nudged open the door and ducked inside. At once he was assaulted by the pungent odor of fresh mash. Taking down a lantern hanging from a nail, he lit it, keeping the flame as low as possible. Moving it about, he glimpsed four oversized stills huddled dimly along one wall. They were entangled in coils of piping that seemed to have no beginning and no end. Along the wall opposite were stacked close to thirty wooden casks. Earthenware jugs were scattered everywhere. Recently cut firewood was piled haphazardly in one corner.

Fargo turned the flame up as high as it would go, waited a second, then hurled the lamp against the pile of wood. The flaming kerosene leaped over the wood, engulfing it. Swiftly, the flames spread across the littered floor to the casks. There was another lamp on a hook. Fargo plucked it down and without bothering to light it, flung it against the casks. At once a great sheet of fire leapt up the casks all the way to the ceiling, then reached out hungrily for the rafters.

The heat was already intense. Holding up his arm to protect his face, he turned and ducked out of the building. Cutting silently through the darkness, he entered the horse barn from the rear, slipped through it and crouched down beside the open door to wait for the flames to be spotted.

It was not long before the flames from the first building spread to the one alongside it. Yet it took a surprisingly long time before anyone in the ranchhouse noticed the raging hell Fargo had planted in their midst. As the flames leaped higher into the night, the compound brightened rapidly, turning the ground beside it as bright as day.

At last, a cry came from the ranchhouse. Will and the others rushed out, the wounded Clampett on their heels.

When Clampett saw the flames, he grabbed hold of a porch post to steady himself momentarily, then began shouting orders to his remaining hands. Will left his father and raced toward the flaming buildings, Clampett and his wife following. Fargo raced back through the barn, came out behind it, and darted across the compound and slipped into the now empty ranchhouse.

In the huge living room he found his gunbelt and Colt flung down on a long table. As soon as he strapped the Colt back on, he snatched up two lighted lamps and darted into the kitchen, hurling both at a wall, he grabbed another lamp and flung it up the stairwell leading to the second floor. Then, slipping back out of the house, he kept to the shadows and kicked his way into the bunkhouse.

From inside it, Fargo heard clearly the shouts and cries of the men and women outside fighting the fire. Peering through a mud-encrusted window, Fargo could see them filling water buckets at the pump and lugging them frantically over to the horsebarn. They were soaking its walls down in an effort to keep the flames from spreading to it. Fargo felt better when he saw Will leading out the horses and the other stock from the barn.

Glancing around the bunkhouse, Fargo realized it was as much a storehouse for moonshine casks as it was a home for Clampett's hands. Lifting a chimney off a lamp, he snapped alight a match with his thumbnail and held it to the wick. He waited a moment for the tongue of fire to cover the wick entirely, then flung the lamp against the wall and darted out of the bunkhouse.

He was halfway to the timber when a figure outlined against the leaping flames cried out and pointed to him. Shouts followed. Fargo kept going. A rifle cracked. Something hot and very heavy pounded into him high up on his right shoulder, spinning him to the ground. Grabbing at the shoulder, he realized the bullet had smashed through, leaving him with a deep flesh wound. Already a thick gout of blood was pulsing from it.

Scrambling to his feet, Fargo flung himself on into the timber just as another rifle shot clipped off a branch inches above his head. Once the pines closed about him, Fargo plunged on through an almost impenetrable darkness—a darkness that all but guaranteed he would lose his pursuers. Cutting swiftly to the right, he headed for the spot where he had left his pinto, doing his best to ignore the searing pain in his shoulder. Soon, the cries of his pursuers had died out completely—and Fargo assumed they had given up on him to return to their blazing compound.

When he reached the pinto, for a moment he felt the ground tip under him alarmingly; but gritting his teeth, he hauled himself up into the saddle and looked back.

The sky over the Clampett compound was a bright orange, the flame's garish light reflected on the undersides of the towering black columns of smoke that pumped into the night sky. Fargo smiled grimly. A new dawn was breaking for the Clampetts.

Now, if he could just make it to Clay Springs and a doctor.

8

Fargo soon discovered that Clay Springs was out of the question.

Recalling what Charlie White Horse had told him, he veered toward the valley. When he came upon the stream, he started up it. A faint hint of dawn was falling over the land when he caught sight of the white rock above him. He put the pinto up onto the bank and started to climb through the timber toward it.

Then things became confusing. He remembered dimly toppling back off the pinto, and the hard blow when his shoulders slammed into the ground. For a while he remembered nothing until he opened his eyes and found his face inches from the pinto's snout. The pony was cropping the grass beside Fargo's head. Nervously, his ears flicking constantly, it lifted his head every now and then to gaze at him.

Fargo reached out for the trailing reins and started to haul himself to his feet. But he couldn't make it. The effort seemed to cut something loose deep within him. He felt the reins slipping through his hand as he plunged back to the ground.

This time he did not feel the ground when he hit it.

Fargo opened his eyes and saw nothing.

He refused to panic, however, despite the smell of raw earth mingled with that of damp, rotting timbers. He lay perfectly still for a moment, aware of the comforting beat of his heart deep in his chest. For a moment there he had thought he might have been buried alive. Then he heard the cool rush of a distant mountain stream. Birdsong echoed in a meadow below him. He relaxed. He recognized the smells now. He was in a sod roofed cabin deep in the mountains.

Abruptly, a door was flung open. A blinding shaft of light exploded into the cabin. Fargo closed his eyes and turned his head away from the sudden brightness—but not before he glimpsed the massive, bent figure entering the cabin. For a moment the man busied himself pulling back heavy wooden shutters from two windows. Through his closed eyelids, Fargo could feel the sunlight pouring like a physical presence into the cabin.

Then, his eyes still closed, he heard heavy footsteps approaching his cot.

"Awake, are you?"

Fargo turned his head and peered up through slitted eyes at the huge mountain man bending over him. "I'm awake, all right. How long have I been here?"

"Goin' on a week now."

Fargo frowned. That was a long time. He must have lost a pint or more of blood before this giant found him. At the moment he felt as weak as a kitten; but his head was clear enough.

The mountain man standing over him smelled of sweaty buckskin, wild onions, and feet that maybe had spent too long in the same boots. His massive head seemed twisted cruelly, as if it had been screwed down onto his shoulders as a clumsy afterthought. It was surmounted by a coonskin cap. The man's long red curls fell to his shoulders and most of his face was covered with a ragged beard. Bright blue eyes blinked cheerfully down at Fargo.

"You'd be Fargo," he said. "Charlie White Horse told me."

"And you're Crooked Elk?"

"Yup. That's what the Crow started to call me after I hurt this here neck of mine. But you can call me Ike. That's my Christian name."

"You mentioned Charlie. Where is he and the girl?"

He grinned. His teeth were surprisingly white. "They took my advice and lit out."

"Oh?"

"You wiped Clampett out single-handed, you did. But now you smashed his hive, he's out with Will searching the hills for you and Charlie. I told Charlie to take Marylou to St. Louis."

"St. Louis?"

"You heard right, pilgrim. That's a fine place for famous western heroes and mountain men to rest up and gain a followin'. Ain't no one there goin' to complain about him having Crow blood. Hell, soon as them newspapermen find that out, Charlie will be famous. Givin' out autographs, and sech. Might even write hisself a book. Yep, him and Marylou'll be safe enough in St. Louis."

Fargo shrugged. Recalling those Beadle dime novels he and Caulder had been reading, Crooked Elk's suggestion make a crazy kind of sense.

"You think maybe you can sit up now?" Crooked Elk asked.

Fargo nodded and threw back the covers. He was dressed only in his long johns. Swinging his feet down, he planted them firmly and stood up. He fixed his sights on a table not too far away and made for that. Reaching it after a few wobbly steps, he pulled out a chair and slumped down into it.

"You done fine," Ike said, moving past him to the big black wood stove in a corner. "You'll be as good as new in no time."

"My pinto. Is it nearby?"

"That purty Ovaro? Sure. Couldn't miss that. But I been keeping it out of sight in the woods, near a stream with plenty of graze. If Clampett sees that pony of yours with the rest of my animals, it'll be a dead giveaway."

"Just so long as he's all right."

"Don't you worry none. That pony of yours is gettin' real fat and sassy." Then Ike grinned at Fargo. "What about you? You hungry?"

That was all it took. As soon as Ike mentioned food, Fargo's stomach flipped in anticipation. "I could eat a bear," Fargo told him.

"Dinner comin' up," the mountain man said, reaching for a pan.

The two men ate out in front of the cabin on the

deal table Fargo helped Ike drag out. The swift stream rushing past the cabin made pleasant enough music, but the flies and mosquitoes were a nuisance. But it would have taken more than that minor inconvenience to detract from the savory magnificence of Ike's muskrat stew.

Large, surprisingly sweet chunks of muskrat swam in a thick broth alongside potatoes, some tender greens Ike had gathered, and wild onions. Ike need not have worried about the stew cooling off any. The onions took care of that. The stew brought sweat to Fargo's brow, a feeling of deep contentment to his belly, and an almost miraculous infusion of energy to his whole being.

They were almost finished when Ike grinned at Fargo and shoved the jug of moonshine toward him. "I see you been looking a mite curious at this here twisted neck of mine."

Fargo took the jug and filled his cup for the second time. It was like drinking lighted kerosene. "Only because it looks like it might be hurtin' you some," he replied.

"That's what most people think. But it don't hurt a bit. It did, though, when it happened."

"Was it a gunshot?"

"Nope. A grizzly."

Fargo waited, aware that Ike was more than anxious to tell Fargo the whole story.

"Used to trap these mountains before the blight of civilization overtook them and the beaver hat went out of style," he began, taking out a clay pipe and beginning to thumb tobacco into the bowl. "It was back in '43. I returned to my camp one bright

October afternoon and found a grizzly rummagin' in my tent. He was really tearing up a storm—'cause he wasn't findin' what he wanted. Something sweet, I reckon. But he had already ruined a passel of beaver skins, so I wasn't as careful as I might have been. I went right in the tent after him. My rifle misfired. Before I could reload, the grizzly swiped at me and took out a chunk of my neck and shoulder. Then, fixing to store me somewhere for a winter snack, I reckon, he dragged me off. But after a while, he lost interest and let me go." Ike laughed. "I allus figured it was my smell. I was a young man then, you see, and I wasn't all that anxious to be eaten alive by no grizzly. In that pure, one-hundred-percent terror that comes to men occasionally, I had shit in my pants."

Fargo smiled. "I can understand that."

Ike shook his head and lit the pipe. "There ain't nothing more intimidatin' than an unfriendly grizzly. I think I'd rather tangle with a drunk squaw."

He puffed for a moment on his pipe and went on.

"I was lucky to be alive. But that's all I was. Alive. When I could move, I figured the only way I could stem the bleeding in my neck and shoulder was to tip my head over and lift my shoulder up close to the wound. Then I bound up my head and shoulder. It stopped the bleedin' all right, and the wound closed. But that meant I couldn't straighten my head again, less'n I wanted to rip open the wound again."

"So it healed that way."

"Yup. It gives me a lopsided view of the world, I admit. There ain't no white woman hankerin' after a

115

freak, but there's plenty of dark-eyed Crow women find pleasure in my bed. So I count my blessin's."

Fargo filled his cup a third time with the moonshine.

"This yours?" he asked Ike.

"Nope. It's Clampett moonshine. It's what's been keepin' the Crow hereabouts off our neck." He grinned at Fargo. "I don't know what they'll do now if Clampett tries to tell them he don't have any more for his thirsty braves."

"You mean that's what the ranchers around here have been using to keep the Crows in line?"

Ike nodded. "It's made a real mess of the Crows. A damn shame."

"That's playing with fire."

"Well, so far, it's done the job. It's kept the Crows too busy to bother the wagon trains using Clay Creek as a jumping off point for Oregon."

Fargo nodded.

Ike cleared his throat nervously. "You mind telling me what that badge in your wallet means?"

"You saw it?"

"You wallet opened up when I was undressing you."

"I'm looking for Johnny Ringo."

"You a lawman?"

"Nope. But that badge was given to me by the man Johnny Ringo killed."

"So you're out to even things."

"Yes."

"I guess I can understand that."

"Why did you ask, Ike? You seemed a mite nervous."

"Well, let's just say before I found these here mountains, I had a somewhat checkered past myself."

"Forget it. There's only one man ı want and that man is Johnny Ringo. Do you know of him?"

"I've heard the name, I think."

"Maybe you can tell me about it. But that'll have to wait. All of a sudden, I'm very, very tired."

Ike looked closely at him and smiled. "You do look washed out some. I think maybe you better go back inside before you overdo it."

"I think so," Fargo agreed, pushing himself to his feet. "But that muskrat stew was worth it, Ike."

"Thought you'd like it."

Fargo went back into the cabin. Almost before he struck the cot, he was asleep.

A strange scratching sound on the door in the middle of the night awakened Fargo. He sat up on the cot as Ike jumped up from his own bed on the floor and pulled the door open. A girl burst in.

Ike hurriedly closed the door and lit a lantern. The girl flung herself into Ike's arms and clung to him, her head buried in his chest. What remained of her bodice was barely enough to cover her breasts. Her skirt had been ripped so badly that her legs, from the knees down, were a mass of ugly bruises.

After a while, she relaxed, pushed away from Ike, and glanced over at Fargo. Her dark hair was wild, matted, her face streaked with dirt. In her eyes Fargo saw mindless terror—the terror of any helpless animal tormented beyond its ability to understand.

Comforting her with soft words, Ike led the girl into the next room, a pantry-like addition where he kept most of his stored roots and vegetables. He came out a moment later.

"She's got a bed in there," he explained.

"She? Who is she, Ike? And what's wrong with her?"

"Her name is Daisy. She belongs to Tarnell's gang. Every now and then she manages to bust loose and turn up here. There ain't much I can do for her. I feed her, gentle her down if I can before they come after her."

"You mean you let them take her back?"

"Can't rightly refuse. She's married to one of Tarnell's men. Finn Larson. Sometimes he drinks too much and begins passing her around—or beating her. But she's his wife, Fargo."

"Hell! I don't see where that has anything to do with it."

"Now, listen here, Fargo. These here mountains belong to Tarnell and those powers that run Clay Springs. There ain't no way I can change that."

"And Clampett's part of that gang."

"I guess that's an accurate enough statement."

"Maybe when they come for this girl, I might have a thing to say about it. Would you object?"

Ike considered a moment. Then his steely blue eyes glinted with anticipation. "Hell no, Fargo. Think maybe I'd like to back your play. I'd say it's about time."

*   *   *

The next morning, bright and early, Daisy left the tiny room, grabbed a bucket and went outside to the stream. She filled the bucket with the ice cold water, and then vanished into the woods. When she returned about half an hour later—though she was still wearing the torn and dirty garments she had arrived in—her person was scrubbed clean. Her hair, no longer matted but combed out and gleaming, had been braided to form a neat crown around her head. Fargo glimpsed hazel eyes, a pert nose, and a sharp, bold chin. A faint dusting of freckles was spread across her scrubbed cheeks.

And an ugly, purpling bruise stood out clearly under one eye.

While Daisy had been off making herself presentable, Ike had cautioned Fargo that breakfast would have to await her return, since she always insisted on cooking for him. Now, as soon as Daisy entered the cabin, she waved the two men out of the cabin and began preparing breakfast. As the two men made themselves comfortable on the low wooden porch, she filled the bright morning air with the sound of banging pans and kettles.

At last breakfast was ready and the two men were allowed back in. Platters of bacon and home fries greeted them, along with salt pork and beans and steaming mugs of black coffee. Each place at the deal table had been set neatly and in a small glass in the center of the table, Daisy had placed some wild flowers. It not only transformed the table, it transformed the room.

Daisy hung back nervously as Ike and Fargo sat down. Ike glanced up at her.

"Sit down, Daisy," he told her.

She hesitated.

"Now, you heard me," he insisted gently.

She sat.

"This here's Skye Fargo, Daisy," Ike said, introducing Fargo. "He's a lawman looking for Johnny Ringo."

She looked at Fargo with sudden concern.

"Do you know Ringo, Daisy?" Fargo asked.

Daisy nodded. "He visits Tarnell often. He just got back a week or so ago."

"Good," said Ike. "We'll talk about it later, Daisy. Fargo might have a few questions."

Daisy frowned. Fargo smiled at her. She returned the smile tentatively.

"Would you like to stay here with Ike, Daisy?" Fargo asked.

The question startled Daisy.

"You don't have to go back if you don't want to," explained Ike. "Fargo and I just decided."

"It will only cause you more trouble if I stay."

"You let us worry about that," said Fargo.

"We'll talk about it later, Daisy," Ike said soothingly. "Now, you just go ahead and eat up. This here breakfast you built for us is fit for a king."

After a hesitant beginning—she was obviously still somewhat alarmed at Ike's announcement—Daisy ate as heartily as did the two men. It was obvious that she was not fed this well at the Tarnell ranch. Once the breakfast was over, the two men were again banished from the cabin. This time they took the opportunity to clean first their Colts, then their rifles.

Ike was the owner of a genuine Hawken rifle, which he kept in superb condition and as Fargo cleaned his Sharps, it brought a low whistle of appreciation from the mountain man. When he finished with his Sharps, Fargo cleaned it, loaded it, then leaned it back against the cabin wall.

Fargo was sipping on some moonshine and Ike was puffing on his clay pipe when Daisy left the cabin, brushed a stray strand of hair off her pale forehead, and approached them. She saw the rifles leaning back against the cabin wall and did not fail to notice that both men had strapped their six-guns to their waists.

"I won't have it," she said.

"You won't have what?" Ike asked.

"I won't have you men getting killed over me. I'll go back like I always do, Ike. It won't be so bad. Just so I get this chance to be away from them bastards for a while. That's all."

"Then you don't mind going back to Finn and the rest of them?" Fargo prodded.

Daisy looked sharply at him. For the first time, she studied his face closely. It was obvious she was trying to find out his motive for wanting her to stay at the cabin with Ike. In her short experience with men, she had learned one thing well—not to trust them. The only reason she trusted Ike was because he was so much older than she.

Fargo, however, was a different matter.

"No, I don't mind," she said. It was obvious she was lying.

"When you burst in last night, you were crying," Fargo reminded her. "There's a bruise on your face still. It's turning purple. You keep going back to them like that, and one day Finn or one of his boys might kill you."

"What do you care?"

"I don't want you for myself, if that's what you're thinking."

"Is that so?"

"Yes, that's so."

Ike broke in then. "Daisy, Fargo's right. Finn might hurt you bad one of these days. And I won't be here to look after you."

She frowned. "I just don't want either of you two to get hurt. That's all."

Fargo smiled at her. "Don't worry. We'll survive."

"When Finn comes after you this time, just go inside and stay there."

Daisy took a deep breath. Then she said, "If you don't kill Finn, he'll come after you—and me. He don't forget."

"We understand," said Ike.

As Daisy fled back inside, Fargo looked at the mountain man. "I'm glad you're so sure we can handle that sonofabitch."

Ike laughed. "Who said I was sure?"

Three days later, about the middle of the morning, a lone rider in a floppy-brimmed hat pulled to a halt in front of Ike's cabin. His lank, straw-colored hair hung down onto his shoulders, and a faint stubble of whiskers covered his chin. His jeans were torn and his buttonless vest had been put on over a filthy undershirt.

Fargo was sitting on the low porch and Ike had come to the doorway as soon as he heard the approaching hoofbeats. Daisy was down by the creek, out of sight behind a clump of willows, washing clothes.

"Howdy, Finn," Ike said.

Finn nodded to Ike, then glanced warily at Fargo. Fargo was obviously a stranger to these parts, and as such immediately suspect. And then again, maybe he had heard about the fellow who had raised such hell with the Clampetts.

Finn looked back at Ike. "Where's Daisy?"

"Down by the stream, washing clothes."

Finn turned the horse and was about to spur the animal toward the stream when Fargo reached for his Colt. Finn saw Fargo's move and yanked his horse back around, his own Colt materializing in his hand. Fargo fired. Finn's Colt went flying.

"What the hell . . . !" Finn cried.

"Daisy's goin' to stay with us for a while," Ike drawled, stepping through the doorway. He was carrying his Hawken.

"That there's my wife," Finn protested. "She goes with me!"

"No, she don't," said Ike. "You been treatin' her too rough. This time I told her she could stay."

The shot had alerted her to Finn's presence and Daisy came running. Her face registering near panic, she darted fearfully around Finn's horse and fled into the cabin.

"Daisy!" Finn cried. "You get your ass out here!"

Daisy poked her head out of the door. "No," she told him. "I'm stayin' here with Ike."

"Like hell you are!"

Feeling braver now, she stepped out and stood beside Ike. "I ain't goin' back! I ain't *ever* goin' to let you beat me again."

"All right then, damnit! I promise you, Daisy. I won't beat on you ever again. An' I won't let no one else do it, either!"

"I don't believe you."

Finn moistened his lips in sudden exasperation. It was beginning to dawn on him that there was a damn good chance he would be going back to the Tarnell ranch without his woman.

"Now, you listen here," he thundered, his face darkening with desperate resolve. "I'm willin' to be sensible. I just gave you my word I wouldn't beat up on you none! But you better haul ass right now, or I'll come back with Tarnell and the rest of the boys. I'll burn this here place to the ground. I'll string up these two varmints by the balls. And damn your hide, I'll make you watch!"

Fargo had heard enough. He strode over to Finn, reached up and dragged him off his horse, then flung him to the ground. Scrambling to his feet, Finn flung himself upon Fargo, who punched him solidly in the face, staggering the man back. Again Fargo charged. Tiring of the game, Fargo clipped Finn on the side of the head with his gun barrel. This time, when Finn hit the ground, he stayed where he was—one hand held up to his head.

"You better kill me now, Mister," Finn rasped harshly. " 'Cause I'm comin' back here, and I ain't comin' alone."

"You mean that?"

"Yer damn right I do."

Fargo picked up Finn's revolver and flung it at him. "You hurt too bad to use this?" he inquired mildly.

Without bothering to answer, Finn snatched up the Colt. Fargo took a step back and dropped his own Colt into his holster. Finn thumbcocked his Colt and pushed himself erect, his face twisted into a grimace of hate. Once on his feet, he closed a finger about the trigger.

Fargo took another step back. "Whenever you're ready," he told Finn.

His eyes cold, Finn flung up his Colt. Fargo drew and fired, his muzzle spitting twice. Both shots came so fast, they seemed to smash into Finn's chest simultaneously. Finn was flung back, his own weapon detonating harmlessly into the air.

Daisy screamed and disappeared back into the cabin.

9

Daisy had flung herself face down on her small cot. She was sobbing. Fargo stopped beside the cot and cleared his throat. Then he placed his hand on Daisy's shoulder.

"Don't cry about that sonofabitch, Daisy. Besides, I didn't have any other choice."

Beside him, Ike took his arm.

"Maybe we better leave her alone for a while."

Fargo nodded. The two men backed out of the tiny room and slumped down at the deal table. Fargo took off his hat and ran his big hands through his raven hair.

"You and Daisy will have to go into Clay Springs for a while until this blows over," he said to Ike.

Ike nodded. "What are you going to do?"

"Take Finn back to his buddies and explain what happened."

"You mean ride in there alone?"

"I'm not about to walk all that distance."

"Fargo, you'd be handing that gang your head on a platter!"

"I don't think so."

"You're crazy, Fargo."

Fargo was patient with Ike. "I'm looking for Johnny Ringo. Daisy said he comes to that ranch once in a while. And I learned a long time ago, Ike: When you do what your enemy don't expect, you got the advantage."

Ike sighed in resignation. "I sure as hell hope so. When you figurin' on leavin'?"

"Soon's I can."

Fargo turned his head to listen. Daisy was no longer crying. He got to his feet, Ike also. Before they could walk into the small room to see how Daisy was, she appeared before them, dabbing her face dry with the back of her hand. She smiled apologetically at them.

"I'm sorry about Finn," Fargo told her.

She dried her eyes with the heel of her hands and smiled hesitantly at them.

"I suppose I shouldn't be cryin' " she said. "Finn was real mean to me."

Ike smiled down at her. "You wouldn't be worth much if you didn't feel something, Daisy."

She nodded sadly. "Finn wasn't always mean. And he promised when he married me, he'd stop drinkin'. He would've, too, if he could've broke away from Tarnell and his gang." She sighed, plucked a torn handkerchief from her sleeve and blew her nose. "He used to be a lot of fun," she said, shaking her head in wonderment.

Fargo accompanied Ike and Daisy half way to Clay Springs, then headed south toward Tarnell's ranch, Finn's horse on a lead behind him, the dead body wrapped in a slicker and tied across the saddle.

An hour or so later, moving through a canyon Ike had directed him to take, Fargo rode over a patch of cap rock, the pony's iron shoes ringing sharply, rounded a bend in the canyon and came upon two mounted Crows sitting their ponies directly in his path.

Fargo pulled up. From behind him he heard the soft thud of unshod ponies. Turning, he saw three, then six, Crows deploying themselves in a line across the canyon floor.

They sat their mounts without moving, ancient flintlocks and lances held across the necks of their patch-colored ponies—as silent as the shadows they cast. Each brave wore a gaily colored mantle, handsome leggings, eagle feathers, and elaborately worked moccasins. In addition to their rifles and lances, they carried bows and arrows. Their hair was gorgeously plumed, with long braids wrapped in strips of otter skin. Some of the braids hung as far as their waists. The hair on the top of their head was stiffened with white clay, imparting to it a sweeping upward curve. Around their necks were hung brass ornaments and pink shells.

The dandies of the Rockies, Fargo reminded himself. But he was not deceived. These savage warriors were not fops. And at the moment they were angry and sullen, their purpose not at all friendly.

A warrior in yellow leggings urged his pony forward, the rest fanning out behind him, every brave riding in the same easy, spraddled fashion. As he got closer, Fargo realized the brave in the lead must be the chief of this war party, judging from the scalp locks depending from his lance. The chief splashed through the shallow pool, and pulled up impassively before Fargo.

The chief had a scar about three inches long over his left eyebrow and another scar on the left side of his chin. There was nothing to read in his face but contempt—that and an almost casual, implacable hatred. His black eyes gleamed with appreciation at what he had pulled in. He was taller than most Crows, almost six feet, with a broad, heavily-muscled upper torso and powerful hands.

The rest of his party pulled up in a semicircle about Fargo, as silent as their chief. Abruptly the chief uttered a few sharp, guttural commands to the braves. They pulled back obediently while one of their number grabbed the reins of Finn's horse. The chief leaned his scarred face close to Fargo's, his eyes boring vindictively into Fargo's.

"You burn firewater ranch!"

Fargo was relieved the Crow chief spoke English. But he was not pleased that this Crow was one of those who had come to depend on Clampett's moonshine. In a way, he could understand the chief's anger. Fargo saw no sense in attempting to deny the charge and figured his only course was to brazen it out. To most Indians a man without courage had no soul—an abomination that must be stamped out as swiftly and finally as a worm.

"Yes," Fargo replied, nodding his head vigorously. "I burn firewater ranch. Firewater not good for the Crow!"

The chief straightened in his saddle, his obsidian

eyes gleaming with fury. "Firewater bring gods to dwell in our lodges," he insisted. "Many visions come then—and the Crow soars like the eagle!"

Fargo knew what the poor fool was admitting—that he and his people had found God in a bottle. "And what happens, Chief," he reminded him, "when all the booze is gone? Who's your master then? Clampett?"

The chief bristled. "Your words say nothing. You do not burn ranch because you are friend to the Crow."

He turned and shouted something to the other braves. They greeted his words with an answering cry that echoed sharply in the canyon. Before Fargo could do anything to stop them, they milled closer about him, grabbing his bowie knife and his Colt. When they lifted his Sharps out from its scabbard, Fargo winced.

Then the chief clipped him on the side of the head with the stock of his rifle, flinging Fargo from his saddle. Fargo landed hard on the flat cap rock of the canyon floor. He tried to spin away, and found himself splashing futilely in the shallow pool. With eager shouts, the rest of the Crows slipped off their ponies and closed about Fargo, cuffing him and kicking at him until he was almost unconscious.

Then they gripped him about the waist from behind and lifted him to his feet. As he sagged in their arms, one brave strode forward and struck him on the side of his head with Fargo's own Colt. Fireworks went off deep inside Fargo's head and he felt his knees turn to water. The brave laughed. Then an open palm, driven with the force of a pile driver, caught his face and spun him around. Fargo lost all control of his limbs. But before he reeled back into the pool, he was held upright as other braves bound his wrists with damp rawhide. Around the rawhide still another brave tied the end of a rope. Dimly, Fargo saw this one mount his pony, still holding on to the rope.

The Indian jerked the rope and Fargo went sprawling face down into the pool. Uttering a shattering war cry, the brave urged his pony to a sudden gallop. Forced to scramble to his feet or be dragged through the water, Fargo regained his feet and was yanked awkwardly through the pool. When he tried to keep up with the pony on the canyon's uneven rock floor, he lost his footing and was dragged, belly-down, over the rocky ground.

The brave pulled up, shouted something to his fellows, then yanked the rope, indicating to Fargo that he should get to his feet. Wearily, painfully, Fargo struggled upright and braced himself. The braves across the pool shouted something to Fargo's captor. The savage laughed, then yanked the rope again. This time, however, Fargo kept his balance and in a glowering fury yanked back—as hard as he could.

He almost dragged the Crow brave off his pony.

The savage shout of appreciation at this show of spirit on Fargo's part filled the canyon. A few grinned at Fargo and lifted their lances in salute to him. Others taunted the brave. This worthy smiled back at Fargo, satisfied. He turned about and urged his pony to a steady walk, jerking Fargo along harshly whenever he showed any signs of slowing up.

The rest of the Crows swung aboard their ponies and galloped past Fargo and his captor, the chief in the lead. Soon, the entire party had settled into an unhurried pace, Fargo and his captor bringing up the rear. It was not easy for Fargo to keep going. He stumbled often and fell more than once. But each time he was unceremoniously jerked back up onto his feet and pulled along.

The Crows were heading toward a cluster of huge rocks that stood like massive sentinels before a wall of rock. The Indians threaded their way through this great stone garden, and Fargo soon found himself traversing a long, sparse flat. The going was somewhat easier here; but now that he was out in the open, the sun poured down on him with unrelenting force.

He was sweating from every pore, his mouth as dry as sawdust. At last they left the flat and followed a game trail. Fargo felt the ground lifting beneath his feet as they rode higher and higher into the mountains. Before long, they entered a thick spruce forest, the cool firs closing over Fargo's perspiring, bleeding figure. Though the slick needles blanketing the forest floor made the going difficult, Fargo was grateful that he was out of reach of the blistering sun.

A little before sundown the group reached the Crow village. Fargo's coming had been announced by advance members of the war party. Ranks of children, old crones, and squaws—eager to welcome him to their village—were lined up in a shrill gauntlet with sticks and pieces of rawhide. By the time he had stumbled through their shrieking, screaming ranks, he was covered with spittle and reeling from several sharp cracks on his skull, while his arms and the back of his neck were a mass of red stripes.

His captor dragged him to a halt before a small lodge, untied the rope holding him, and shoved him inside. Once Fargo found himself alone, he hunched up in the darkness and went to work with his teeth on the rawhide strands. They had tightened around his wrist like bands of steel.

He had not got very far when the entrance flap was thrown back and John Clampett strode in, his gaunt face radiating the satisfaction he felt at seeing Fargo in his present condition. Clampett held a rifle in one hand and his eyes were bright with madness.

"Now, you Godforsaken sonofabitch!" he cried. "You will see what your damnable interference has reaped! You are going to burn—to hell and beyond!"

Fargo simply looked at him.

Clampett took a single stride closer. "You killed my son!"

"We all go sometime, Clampett. All the same, I am sorry about your boy. But you know as well as I do—it was kill or be killed."

"Yes! And now, praise be to a merciful God, it is *your* turn to die."

"Then so be it."

That Fargo seemed unmoved by this threat evidently upset Clampett.

"Maybe you won't feel so satified with yourself,

Fargo, when I tell you that not all my moonshine was destroyed in that fire. And tonight—while you burn—there will be many Crows filling the night with their cries as they celebrate your burning."

"Like yapping coyotes. And you'll be joining. You should be real proud of yourself, Clampett."

Clampett kicked Fargo.

At that moment, the chief who had captured Fargo stepped into the lodge. He pulled up beside Clampett and fixed him with a cold, imperious stare, then indicated with a sharp movement of his head that Clampett should get out.

With remarkable speed, Clampett turned and left.

"I am Tall Bear," the chief told Fargo. "You will die slowly this night. And then Clampett will build a new firewater ranch for the Crow. This, Clampett promise."

"And if he does," Fargo replied, "it will be the death of the Crow. The firewater will steal their manhood. They will become like children. The Crow braves will crawl upon the earth like worms. Like an evil wind, the enemy of the Crow will sweep over them."

Fargo could see that his words impressed Tall Bear. But this, of course, only made the chief more stubborn.

"Your words are dust on the wind," he told Fargo.

"Bring in the other chiefs. I will talk to them."

"I am the foremost chief. I do not need other chiefs to tell me what I must do."

"No, the firewater will tell you. And Clampett. It is Clampett who tells Tall Bear what to do."

Tall Bear's face darkened. "You speak lie!"

Fargo caught Tall Bear's eyes and held them. "Tall Bear knows I speak the truth. Clampett and his firewater will destroy his people."

The chief spun about and fled the tipi. Fargo's medicine was too strong for him, it seemed. But as he went back to chewing on the rawhide, Fargo sensed he had pushed Tall Bear too far; by this time Tall Bear was probably a full-blown alcoholic.

And Fargo had never known one to give up his bottle willingly.

As soon as Ike and Daisy left Fargo, Ike began noticing numerous Crow sign. At once he realized that Fargo would never reach the Tarnell ranch. So he sent Daisy on alone once they were in sight of Clay Springs. Daisy had assured him she would be all right, that Ma Devlin would be glad to take her in again. She always needed fresh girls.

Traveling fast through familiar country, Ike arrived at Tall Bear's camp a little before sundown. Dismounting on a bluff overlooking it, he hunkered down and peered carefully at the Crow encampment. It was a small, pathetically mean camp scattered beside a shallow stream no wider than a brook. There were at most only ten lodges and the ground around each of them was littered with refuse. It was the camp of a band of Crow that had given in almost entirely to the effects of alcohol. At sight of it, Ike felt once again a deep sadness. He had known the Crows before the coming of the white man and his devilish brew. And he had seen how the magic they found in his alcohol had sapped their ancient wisdom and strength, replacing it with a wild and uncontrollable dissipation.

It was rum that would wipe out the Indians, not the soldiers and not the settlers. Of this, Ike was certain.

As he watched the camp, he found no sign of Fargo and was about to conclude that his suspicions had been groundless when he saw Tarnell and two of his hands ride into camp, escorting a small covered wagon. Tarnell was greeted by Clampett and Tall Bear. At once Clampett was escorted to a small, ragged-looking lodge on the edge of the camp. A moment later Fargo was dragged out in front of the lodge by one of Tarnell's hands and worked over for a while. When the hands had exhausted themselves, Fargo was propped up in front of the lodge, his back to a post driven into the ground, and left.

A quick scrutiny of the rest of the camp told Ike all he needed to know. A large stake was being set up in the middle of the camp and the rest of the Crows were crowding excitedly around the wagon as Tarnell's hands passed out the bottles of moonshine they had brought with them.

Ike waited until night. Then he tethered his mount to a sapling and moved down the slope until he was much closer to the camp. Ducking into a juniper thicket, Ike pushed aside the branches and peered through them at the excited Indians staggering exuberantly about the encampment, most of them with bottles in their hands.

There was frantic activity in the central area of

the camp. A fire was being built into a bonfire around the stake Ike had noticed earlier.

Fargo was still sitting up in front of the tepee, his hands and feet bound together in front of him. As Ike watched, an old crone with a bowl of something in her hand came up and stood over him for a moment, hurling abuse on him. Then, as Ike watched, she dumped the bowl's contents over Fargo's head. Even at this distance Ike thought he could hear the old squaw's shriek of laughter.

Looking beyond the camp, Ike caught sight of the Indian's pony herd. That meant there would be an ancient Crow or two on guard near the ponies. He left the juniper and, moving back up through the timber, came down on the far side of the ponies. On his belly the last fifty yards, Ike inched toward the small herd.

There was only one old Indian on guard, his head nodding over an ancient flintlock, a bottle of moonshine in his right hand, his back to a boulder. The ponies seemed to be getting increasingly restless at the insistent drumming and the piercing cries of the drunken Indians. To Ike's surprise, Fargo's Ovaro was milling about with the other ponies, but the Indians, in their eagerness to partake of the moonshine, had failed to unsaddle the pony.

Ike was pleased. It was nice when these inebriated bastards made it easy for him.

Ike approached the old Indian from behind the boulder. When he reached it, he stood up, reached over and swung his left forearm around, catching the Indian under his chin. The move was quick enough to stifle any outcry. With the brave's neck stretched back, Ike drew his Green River swiftly across it. The Indian loosened and Ike let him collapse forward into his own gore, then sheathed his knife and waited patiently for the first rush of blood to stop. He would not have guessed the old Crow could have had so much blood in him. At last he dragged the dead Indian over onto his side, then hefted him onto his back.

Flattening himself on the ground with the corpse draped over him—and doing his best to ignore the warm blood that still trickled sluggishly from the old man's neck—Ike approached the encampment, heading for the tepee where he had last seen Fargo. He kept to the shadows and moved only when he was certain he could not be seen. It was the dogs he feared, and soon two of them darted at him out of the darkness.

Ike put his head down and lay still, allowing the dead Indian to cover his head and shoulders. The dogs sniffed busily about him, but the familiar smell of the Indian satisfied them, and soon they left him. Ike continued to the tepee, crawled around behind it, lifted the hide and crawled inside. Once safely in the lodge, he nudged the dead Indian off him, then crept to the entrance and peered out. Fargo was sitting up, busily gnawing on the rawhide that bound his wrists.

Beyond him the savages were dancing wildly, their shrieks puncturing the night. Looking closer, Ike saw Clampett and Tarnell and three of his men dancing just as heartily, each one with a Crow squaw clinging to him. In a moment, Ike realized, they would be ready for the evening's climax and would be coming for Fargo.

A Crow squaw darted out of the darkness. She was holding a blazing arrow. With a shriek she plunged its flaming head into Fargo's chest, extinguishing the flame with Fargo's blood. With a triumphant cry she spun about and went racing back to the bonfire, the arrow held triumphantly over her head. She had just counted coup.

Reaching back, Ike flung the dead Indian out beside Fargo. Fargo turned, astonished. Reaching out quickly, Ike sliced through the rawhide strips binding Fargo's wrists and ankles. Fargo immediately darted past him into the tipi.

"Massage your wrists and ankles," Ike called after him.

Ike turned the Indian around and propped him up against the post, so that he was in approximately the same position Fargo had been in. In the darkness the slumped figure could barely be made out, especially when looking away from the camp's blazing bonfire. At least this was what Ike was counting on. He ducked back into the teepee. Fargo was crouched in the darkness, waiting for him.

Fargo found it difficult to believe his good fortune—or Ike's incredible audacity. No question about it. The mountain man had just saved his life.

"Ike, you crazy sonofabitch!" Fargo exclaimed softly, "Where in hell did you come from?"

Ike laughed. "Never mind that. I just saw that squaw stick an arrow into you. You hurt bad?"

"She was too drunk to drive it in far enough," Fargo replied, still vigorously rubbing the blood back into his wrists and ankles. "Besides, the flames cauterized it."

"You ready to move out?"

"Not yet," Fargo said.

"What's the matter?"

"Tall Bear's tepee. Can you tell which one it might be?"

With a frown, Ike turned and peeked out through the entrance. For a moment he studied the layout of the Crow camp. Turning back around, he said, "It's probably the big one across the camp, on the other side of the bonfire. The one with all the coup sticks in front of it."

Fargo nodded. "Then let's go," he said.

"You got a reason?"

"I sure as hell have. My Sharps."

Ike nodded and led the way out through the rear of the tepee. With Ike in the lead, they moved swiftly through the darkness, around to the other side of the encampment. They moved cautiously, keeping low. Suddenly, out of the shadows, a Crow warrior leaped toward Fargo, his war cry completely lost in the throbbing drumbeat that filled the night. Fargo only had time to duck. The Crow—drunk, but still incredibly strong—caught Fargo around his neck and twisted him cruelly about.

Grappling desperately, Fargo managed to wrest the brave's hatchet from his grasp, but already weakened considerably by his ordeal, Fargo found himself being borne relentlessly to the ground. Abruptly, he was free as Ike grabbed the Crow about the neck, effectively choking off any further outcry. Before the Crow could recover, Ike buried his knife in the Indian's chest. It was over that quickly, and they continued on through the night toward Tall Bear's lodge.

Ike stood guard outside as Fargo lifted the skirts of the teepee and ducked into it. Fargo found a candle and lit it. Holding the flickering light aloft, he saw his Sharps lying beside a bed of pine boughs, along with his Colt. He dropped the Colt into his holster and grabbed his Sharps. But he was still without a knife. He caught sight of a sheathed knife hanging from a strip of rawhide. He snapped the rawhide and slipped the blade from its sheath. It was long and wickedly curved, and as sharp as a razor. Fargo wielded it a couple of times, admiring its fine balance. Satisfied, he sheathed it and hung it from his gunbelt. Then he ground out the candle with his boot and left the tepee.

"Let's go," he said.

Without a word, Ike turned and led the way through the darkness. Before long, still undetected, they had circled the encampment and were within sight of the pony herd. Ike pointed to a cluster of ponies at the rear of the nervously milling remuda.

"There's your pinto," he said. "On the other side. It's still saddled."

Fargo saw the Ovaro and nodded, pleased. At the same time he realized that only Indians half-crazed with alcohol could be this slipshod. Fargo turned to Ike. "Where's your mount?" he asked.

"Back up the slope, on the other side of the camp."

"I'll give you as much time as I can."

"What are you plannin', Fargo?"

"Can't you guess? This herd looks about ready to jump over the moon."

Ike grinned. He knew exactly what Fargo had in mind. With a quick wave, he turned and vanished into the night.

Fargo waited for at least ten minutes. Then he moved slowly and carefully through the nervous herd to the side of his pinto. The horse recognized Fargo at once. He greeted Fargo by lifting his head in a sudden, quick bobbing motion. Fargo patted the Ovaro gently on the neck and led him to the rear of the herd. Then he cut the rope corral and mounted up.

As a result of the terrific din that now came from the Indian encampment, the herd was becoming increasingly skittish. Twice Fargo thought he heard the cries of someone dying. At one time a woman's high, keening scream cut through the night like a scalpel. And still the dancing and the outcry continued without letup. The Crows and their white friends were having themselves quite a toot. Before long—if their alcoholic fog allowed them to remember what they were about—they would be coming for Fargo. And in their present state, perhaps they would not even notice that they were burning one of their own tribesmen.

But Fargo had already decided it was time to end the party. Looking about him, he saw that the ponies were on the verge of panic. It would not take much to send them on a mindless stampede through the night.

Fargo took out his Colt and sent a shot into the

night, close over the heads of the pony herd. The ponies took off almost as one animal, charging at the encampment, their tails straight out. Clapping his heels to the flanks of his pinto, Fargo followed the herd, sending two more thunderous charges from his Colt into the air, imparting still more impetus to the terrified animals as they surged on through the darkness. In a moment they had burst upon the startled encampment.

Bent low over the neck of his pinto, Fargo kept close behind the herd. Picking targets at random in the camp about him as he charged through, he fired with devastating accuracy. One Crow with a rifle went down, and Clampett was reaching for his six-gun when Fargo's round caused him to pitch forward into the fire. Another white man beside him, a chunky, heavyset fellow, went down as well. An arrow whistled over Fargo's head and someone detonated a flintlock off to his right. But by then he was already through the encampment and it was too late for the befuddled Indians to do anything but watch him and their ponies disappear into the darkness.

Fargo looked back, saw no pursuit, and holstered his Colt. Until they recovered them, the Crows would have to go on foot. A terrible disgrace for a Crow—or any other horse Indian. It was just as Fargo had warned Tall Bear. Clampett's firewater would turn his people into worms crawling over the earth, ripe targets for their enemies.

10

As soon as they judged themselves to be a safe distance from the Crows, Fargo and Ike made camp and rode into Clay Springs late the next day. The two men left their mounts at the livery, then freshened up at the barber shop and registered at the hotel. There were only two small rooms left. They took them, hauled their gear up the stairs, then went to Ma Devlin's place in search of Daisy.

Ma Devlin ran a saloon and cathouse, all in one. She called it the Sultan's Palace. As soon as Fargo followed Ike through the batwings, he was impressed. The saloon boasted a huge mahogany bar, behind which ran an equally long mirror with shelves of bottled liquor—imported wines as well as a fine assortment of whiskeys. Roulette wheels and faro tables crowded hard upon the bar, with the poker tables in the rear.

The place was densely packed and it took some doing for Fargo and Ike to push through the noisy crush to the satin-draped parlor beyond. This place was crowded too, but not so densely. There was a smaller bar in the far corner, where four customers were quietly sipping their drinks, scantily clad girls hanging onto them. On a stand just under a lush, wall-length portrait of a nude woman reclining under a cottonwood, there glowed a mineral-oil lamp with a red bull's-eye shade. The faint odor of incense hung in the air. A curtained doorway led from the parlor.

Without going any farther, Fargo knew what he would find beyond the doorway: a dim corridor, and, on each side, curtained cubicles, perhaps no more than five feet wide, each crib containing a straw mattress, a rocking chair, a commode, and most certainly a young girl or woman.

"I told Daisy we'd be after her," said Ike as he came to a halt and looked around. "I didn't want her getting back to her old profession. I figured Ma would let her help out in the saloon here."

Fargo nodded. But he didn't feel as optimistic as Ike did.

He had known more than a few women in the profession. They protested a hell of a lot, he found, and many of them cut their own throats when they got too ragged for the clientele—but there was sure as hell never a shortage of them in any town he had entered. And he knew madams. They always knew a good girl when they saw one coming.

Maybe, after what she had been through with Finn Larson, Daisy had been only too glad to come home to Ma Devlin.

As the two men stopped at the small bar, a heavily rouged woman emerged from the hallway and came toward them, a careful, wary smile on her round face. She was huge, her bosom more than ample. Yet she carried herself as lightly as if she were still a slim young thing at the beginning of her career.

"Well, hello there, Ike, you old buffalo!" she cried. "Where you been keepin' yourself?"

Ike grinned at her. "Howdy, Ma. I see business is good."

"Some things never go out of style, Ike. You ought to know that."

Then Ma looked up at Fargo, expecting an introduction. Ike introduced her to Fargo and Fargo could see at once that the name had special meaning for her. Fargo smiled politely and touched the brim of his hat to her.

"Well, now," Ma said, grinning up at Fargo. "Looks like it'll take more than one girl to haul this here feller's ashes, and that's the God's truth!"

Ike cleared his throat nervously. "Ma, we come here lookin' for Daisy. I sent her on yesterday. Did she get in here all right?"

Ma's face clouded, but her smile held up bravely. "That's why I came over soon's I saw you," she said.

"Out with it, Ma."

"Johnny Ringo was in here last night. He started to work over one of my girls. I wasn't here, or I would've went after him. And I ain't got me a good bouncer since my last one lit out."

"You mean Daisy went up against Johnny Ringo?" Fargo asked.

Ma nodded unhappily. "I put her in charge of the place. She did her best to protect the girl, but Johnny hit her, hit her hard. Then, from the way I heard it, she threatened Johnny, told him there was someone after him, someone who would make him pay."

"Go on," said Ike, his voice heavy with apprehension.

"Johnny got real mad. He shook Daisy something firece until she told him who she meant." Ma looked directly at Fargo then. "When she told him it was you, mister—Skye Fargo—Johnny rode out and took her with him."

Fargo swore softly.

"There's something else," Ma went on.

"Go on, Ma," Ike prompted. "We're listening."

Ma moistened her lips nervously. "Johnny said, if this guy Fargo still had that badge and wanted to see Daisy alive again, he could find Johnny at Tarnell's ranch." Again Ma turned to Fargo and spoke to him directly. "Johnny says he'll be waiting for you."

Fargo glanced unhappily at Ike. "Damn, we never should have told Daisy I was after Ringo."

Ike nodded gloomily. "Let's get out of here," he said.

The two men thanked Ma, then left her place. It was late. A few street lamps were already lit and still the little town was bustling with activity, the main street filled with settlers' wagons rumbling through. Whatever its human cost, the use of moonshine to keep the Crow off balance seemed to have worked.

At least for now.

The two men halted a few stores down and looked at each other.

"What now?" Ike said.

"I go after Johnny Ringo," Fargo told him. "I still got that badge, and now I got one more good reason for nailing him."

"You know where Tarnell's place is?"

"If it ain't moved from where you told me it was before."

"It ain't."

"When you going?"

"First thing. Sunup."

Ike nodded. "Good idea. I'll be ready."

"You ain't goin', Ike. I want to travel fast and light. And it's me Ringo's after, not you. Besides, you'd only confuse things."

Ike looked at Fargo for a long while, then shrugged. "Guess maybe you're right at that."

"I know I am, Ike."

The two men headed for the hotel. Fargo was looking forward to his solitary bed and the sleep he would need if he was going to make it safely back through Crow country to nail Johnny Ringo.

He tried not to think of what Daisy was going through at that moment.

Dawn was cracking open the eastern sky when Fargo entered the livery. The boy cleaning out the stalls looked up when he entered.

"You Skye Fargo?" he asked.

"That's me."

"I got a note for you," he said, reaching back into the pocket of his Levi's.

He handed Fargo the note, then went back to pitching fresh hay into one of the stalls. Fargo unfolded the note and read:

Fargo,

I no how to get to Tarnell's ranch alot quicker than you. So I am riding out to-nite. I think I can talk sens to Tarnell or Ringo. I jest don't want Daisy hurt by them bastids.

Give me a day or too, if I don't cum back by then, mebbe you better cum after me.

Ike

Fargo crumpled the note and flung it into a corner. Ike would be no match for those butchers, big as he was. Fargo knew what the mountain man had been thinking: if Fargo were to go in after Ringo with his gun blazing, there was always a chance Daisy would get hit by a stray bullet.

"Saddle that Ovaro," Fargo told the stable boy. "I'll be right back."

Hurrying from the stable, he crossed to the hotel for the rest of his gear. He would not give Ike those two days he wanted. The most time Fargo would give him were the hours he had taken that night.

When Fargo returned a few moments later with his gear, the stable boy gave him the news. Word was sweeping town that the Crows were pulling out—something about their chief, Tall Bear, being in disgrace and his magic gone for good.

As Fargo rode out of town minutes later, this news gave him some comfort and later accounted for the lack of trouble he experienced riding through Crow country.

It was late the same day when he rode cautiously out onto an open flat still being hammered by the fierce late-afternoon sun. The pinto surprised a jackrabbit and sent it sailing in great, bounding leaps. Then, rounding a huge, thrusting shoulder of rock, Fargo caught sight of Tarnell's ranch on the far side of the flat—three buildings, a ranchhouse, a bunkhouse, and a barn. The ranch had been set down in front of a massive foothill whose flanks were covered with a thick pelt of timber.

A stream cut just in front of the ranch yard. For anyone to approach the ranch from the west, he would have to cross the long open flat, then ford the stream—all the while in plain sight of the ranch's occupants. Fargo decided it would be best to flank the ranch, coming at it from the timbered foothills.

He pulled his pinto about and disappeared back behind the shoulder of rock, then headed east toward the foothills.

The moon had not yet risen above the peaks when Fargo left the cover of the timber and darted across the dark ground to the rear of the bunkhouse. He carried only his knife and Colt. In close quarters, his rifle would be of little use.

The bunkhouse appeared empty. To make sure, Fargo pushed open the door and searched the low, dark building thoroughly. He found no one. Leaving the bunkhouse, he darted lightly through the darkness to a corner of the ranchhouse. The windows were bright with lantern light, and Fargo could hear the frequent barks of harsh laughter that came from within. As Fargo watched, a shadow moved across one of the windows.

Fargo glanced over at the barn. The big doors were wide open. He watched the dark cavity until he was certain no one was crouched there, waiting. Fargo frowned. Johnny knew Fargo was coming for him. So where were the guards? Had Ike actually managed to calm down Ringo and Tarnell, take the girl, and clear out?

The front door of the ranchhouse swung open. Light flooded out onto the littered yard. A man Fargo did not recognize appeared in the doorway and emptied a slops jar. The sound of its heavy contents slapping the ground came to Fargo clearly— along with its pungent stench. The fellow stepped back out of the doorway and pulled the door shut behind him.

Fargo allowed himself to relax. Apparently, those inside the house suspected nothing; they would not have allowed that fellow to expose himself that carelessly if they had. Fargo waited awhile longer, then moved closer to the front window and flattened himself against the wall.

He could hear the active hum of voices inside and tried to figure how many there were. He was pleased that he did not hear Daisy's voice. But at last, unable to rely on voices alone to determine how many men were inside, he moved closer to one of the windows and peered carefully into the front room. He caught a glimpse of five men around a table playing cards. One of the players was the same man who had just emptied the slops jar. He was obviously a full-blooded Crow, his long braided hair extending from under his hat brim all the way to his waist.

As the five men played, Johnny Ringo emerged from a bedroom. He paused for a moment to pull his belt tight and buckle it. Then, stretching lazily, he sauntered over to watch the game. There was an unstoppered whiskey bottle on the table. He picked it up and pulled on it a couple of times.

As Ringo stood by the table, Fargo heard him address one of the players as Tarnell. Fargo looked closely at the man. At once his memory was jogged to life. Tarnell had been one of those white men Fargo had seen standing beside Clampett when he drove the Indian ponies through the Crow camp. He remembered hitting both Clampett and Tarnell. At the moment Tarnell's left arm was in a sling, but it didn't seem to be hindering his card playing any. The rancher was heavyset, with an unruly shock of gray hair, a fleshy face, and close-set, mean eyes. As Fargo watched, the man flung down his hand in disgust and reached for the bottle.

A thought just occurred to Fargo and he looked back at the door leading from the bedroom Ringo had just left. Ringo had been buckling his belt as he walked from it, a look of sleepy satisfaction on his face. Groaning inwardly, Fargo left the window and ducked swiftly around to the rear of the ranch house. A dim lantern light shone feebly through one of the windows, the one that looked out from the bedroom Johnny Ringo had just left.

Wiping the grime off the windowpane, Fargo saw Daisy lying down on a huge brass bed. Naked, with only a torn, moth-eaten blanket thrown over her slim body, she was staring up at a corner of the ceiling, tears streaming down her angry face. Ike had not taken her from this place, after all. So where in hell was he?

Fargo moved quickly to the next window. The pane on this one was also encrusted with dirt. As soon as he was able to see into the room, he found himself looking at a wall hung with a tangle of harness, bridles and reins. In one corner, two old saddles were huddled forlornly against each other.

The door to the tack room was ajar, and Fargo could see into the bedroom where Daisy was and beyond that, he could see the door leading out to the room where they were playing poker. The yellow band of light streaming through the door into the tack room slanted onto a pile of flour sacks in a corner. Fargo glanced into the corner and was about to look away when his eye caught something.

Fargo groaned and looked closer.

Now that his mind told him what he might be looking at, his eyes were able to pick out the curiously twisted head and massive shoulders of Ike's sprawled body. What had appeared momentarily as a disordered pile of flour sacks was in reality Ike's huge torso sprawled naked in the corner. As Fargo's eyes got accustomed to the dim light, he was able to make out the long, raw stripes that traversed the length of Ike's body. Great ribbons of flesh had been ripped away, starting from Ike's shoulders and extending down past his thighs. And where Ike's nose should have been, there was only a gaping hole.

Fargo stepped back from the window and tried frantically to raise it. But it held fast. Dirt and time had combined to wedge it firmly shut. Fargo tried again, his desperate rage giving him a strength that surprised him. The sash gave only a little, but it was enough. Thrusting the barrel of his Colt in under the sash, he levered the sash up an inch or two higher. Then, holstering his Colt, he grabbed the sash with both hands and heaved upward. It gave at least three inches. Fargo heaved again, exerting every last ounce of strength he had and slowly, inexorably, he raised the sash high enough to let him boost himself into the room.

Slowly Fargo eased the tack room door shut. Then he bent over Ike's body. The man was awesomely still. He rested his ear on the man's ravaged chest and heard the faint, steady drum of a heartbeat. Gently, he took Ike's shoulders and shook him.

"Ike," he whispered. "It's Fargo! Can you hear me?"

Ike's head nodded slightly. The hole where his mouth should have been twisted grotesquely. A dim, grating sound issued from it. "That you . . . Fargo?"

"It's me, all right. I'll get you out of this. Just hang on!"

"No, Fargo . . . please!"

"What is it, Ike?"

"I told Ringo you was dead, killed by the Crow. Daisy backed me up. Ringo won't be expectin' you."

"Nice going, Ike. I was wondering about that. Now, lie still, and I'll open the window further and ease you out of here."

"No! Forget about me. I'm finished. Save Daisy!"

"You're not finished, Ike."

Ike reached up a claw of a hand and grabbed

Fargo's shoulder. Holding it with a fierce, surprising strength, he pulled Fargo closer. "Tarnell and Ringo did this to me. That Crow ranch hand of Tarnell's showed them how. Get them for me, Fargo. Please . . !"

"I will. That's a promise. Lie quiet now, while I tend to these butchers."

"Sure, Fargo. I'll lie quiet . . . now."

Ike closed his eyes. He seemed to sigh. The long, tormented body sagged. Again Fargo leaned close. This time he could no longer hear the mountain man's faintly beating heart. It had stopped. A coldness—like a chill wind—brushed Fargo. He shivered fitfully and drew back from Ike's dead body.

Then he drew his Colt and stood up.

He had not closed the tack door all the way. Now he eased it open just a crack. Through it, he saw Tarnell entering Daisy's bedroom. Tarnell turned and closed the bedroom door behind him, then walked over and sat down on the edge of Daisy's bed, his back to Fargo. He had a jug of moonshine in his good hand and was offering some of it to Daisy.

Fargo pushed the door open wider. It creaked. Tarnell began to turn. Fargo strode out swiftly and brought his Colt down on Tarnell's head, snatching the jug from him as Tarnell collapsed to the floor.

Daisy only just managed to keep herself from crying out in surprise.

"Ike!" she whispered. "How's Ike?"

"He's dead."

He saw the light go out in her eyes. Her face

became a bitter mask as a tear rolled down her cheek. He patted her comfortingly on the arm.

"Get dressed," he whispered. "Hurry."

She nodded.

As Daisy dressed, Fargo went to the door and opened it a crack. The five men were still at the poker table. He returned to Daisy.

Leaning close, he whispered, "Go out through the window in the tack room. I'll give you time to make it to the barn before I make my move here."

"You'll get them, won't you, Fargo?" she whispered urgently. "For what they did to Ike! Please!"

"Yes," he assured her. "Now, get going."

Swiftly, she kissed his cheek, then fled into the tack room. He waited until she had slipped out through the open window. Then he flattened himself against the wall alongside the bedroom door and waited.

His intention was to give Daisy enough time to reach the barn safely, but in less than a minute, one of the poker players shouted in to Tarnell. Since there was no response, he called again—louder. The Crow sitting beside him made a pungent crack in pidgin English. The others laughed. The poker player flung down his cards and strode toward the bedroom.

Pushing the door all the way open, he walked in. Fargo nudged the door shut behind him just as the man saw Tarnell's sprawled body. He spun then and saw Fargo, but before he could utter a word, Fargo clubbed him. The sound the barrel made as it crunched into the man's skull was almost loud enough to alert those in the other room.

At that moment Tarnell regained consciousness. When he saw Fargo and the crumpled poker player on the floor in front of him, he opened his mouth to cry out. In one swift motion, Fargo brought up his Colt, aimed and fired. Part of the man's face disappeared, the floor under his head turning a dark crimson.

Startled voices erupted from the next room. Fargo heard a table overturning and the sound of a lamp crashing to the floor. Grabbing the lamp from the top of the dresser, Fargo kicked the door open and flung it at the four men. He caught the Crow belt high. The Crow staggered back, his torso exploding into a whirling, flapping torch. Flames from his spinning body leapt out, to join those other flames already racing across the room from the lamp that had smashed to the floor a second earlier.

Standing calmly in the doorway, Fargo fired through the roaring flames at the other three, who by now were stampeding toward the door, Johnny Ringo in the lead. Fargo snapped a shot at Ringo, but the outlaw vanished into the night, the round biting off a piece of the doorframe.

The other two men were not so lucky. Before they reached the doorway, it became a swirling mass of flame as the cold night wind sucked the hot air out through the door. The intense heat drove the men back toward Fargo. Fargo held up his left arm to protect his eyes from the awesome heat and punched off two more quick shots. Both men staggered, then fell back into the flames. They began writhing in the midst of the inferno like damned souls.

Fargo bolted back into the bedroom. The fellow he had dropped with his gun barrel a moment before was crawling on his hands and knees toward the tack room. Fargo kicked the man out of the way, ducked into the room, and flung himself through the window, carrying shards of glass and pieces of broken sash with him.

He landed lightly, rolled over, and jumped to his feet. Screams came from behind him. He looked back. The man he had kicked out of the way was trying to pull himself out through the flaming tackroom window. He looked like a giant worm trying to wriggle out from under a searing foot. Fargo aimed carefully and fired. The round caught the doomed man high on the forehead and hurled him back into the thundering inferno.

Fargo raced away from the flaming ranchhouse, heading for the barn where he had sent Daisy. Somewhere out here, he knew, was Johnny Ringo—the man he had ridden so many long miles to apprehend. He did not want to let him escape again. But for the moment it was Daisy's safety that concerned him.

He was almost to the barn when a powerful black charged out, Johnny Ringo in the saddle. Daisy was flung across his pommel. As Ringo swept toward Fargo, Fargo flung himself to one side. Ringo punched two shots at him, but Fargo did not dare return the fire. He could not risk hitting Daisy.

Flinging one last shot back at Fargo, Ringo disappeared into the night.

Scrambling to his feet, Fargo raced for the timber where he had tethered his pinto.

11

Fargo caught sight of Johnny Ringo before he crossed the long flat. The pinto served Fargo well, plunging through the stream and racing across the moonlit flat at a speed that kept Fargo within striking distance of the fleeing Ringo as the heavily laden black labored under the weight of both Ringo and Daisy.

By sunup, Fargo was still within a mile of Ringo; it was obvious now that he was making a beeline for Clay Springs. Within sight of the canyon, Fargo glimpsed Ringo just entering it. He pulled up and gave the pinto a chance to blow. Chances were that Ringo would make his stand in those rocks. And with Daisy as a hostage and shield, Ringo would more than likely be able to call most of the shots.

But all Fargo could do was ride into the canyon and draw Ringo's fire, hoping for the best. Johnny Ringo had been pretty damn lucky so far. His luck couldn't last forever.

The sun was halfway to noon when Fargo clattered into the canyon and began to cut through it. He kept close to the wall, his eyes peering up at the rims, his Sharps loaded and ready. He was cutting around a boulder, heading across an open stretch with little or no cover on either side of him, when he caught sight of Ringo's black stretched out pitiably in the glare of the hot sun. Its chest and flanks covered with dried foam, the horse was still thrashing feebly. Ringo had not even bothered to unsaddle the beast. Judging from its condition, the black must have given out on Ringo not too long ago.

Dismounting beside the black, Fargo loosened the cinch and pulled off the saddle. Then he peeled off the saddle blanket. The horse was in the shadows by this time, and Fargo was hoping it would recover. As he stood back, he heard Daisy's faint cry of warning from high above. He dodged to one side a second before Ringo's round exploded at his feet. As the shot echoed in the canyon, Fargo snatched the Sharps from its scabbard and sighted on the canyon rim. He caught the dim figure of Ringo outlined against the sky and squeezed the trigger. A section of rock just below the rim exploded. Ringo ducked back and out of sight.

Daisy's warning cry, Fargo realized, had more than likely saved his life.

Leaping astride his pinto, he spurred him in under the rim, and hastily dismounted. Deciding against trying to haul his Sharps up that steep a climb, Fargo dropped it back into his scabbard, checked the load in his Colt, then plunged up the slope, looking for a way to the crest. He found a narrow game trail and started up. A hundred or so feet up from the floor of the canyon, the trail petered out and he found his route blocked by a sheer plane of rock.

Reaching for a handhold in a narrow crack, he pulled himself up and then across the rock face. Once safely above it, he reached out for a projecting rock and used it to pull himself up into a narrow niche. Just as he reached the niche, the piece of rock he had used for a handhold came loose. Spewing tiny pebbles out ahead of it, the rock went bounding down the face of the cliff. In seconds it had collected enough debris and loose gravel to transform itself into a small avalanche.

But it was the racket that worried Fargo. He pushed himself deeper into the niche and waited for any sign that Ringo might have heard the slide. He did not have long to wait. Just above him Ringo's rifle cracked. The round struck a brow of rock over Fargo's head and ricocheted off into the canyon. Two more shots followed in rapid succession, but each round whined harmlessly off the covering rock.

Fargo remained perfectly quiet, pressing himself into the niche. There was a good chance that Ringo was shooting at the spot from which he believed the avalanche had started simply as a precaution, since it was doubtful Ringo could see Fargo from where he was. For a while longer, Ringo's bullets whined around Fargo like infuriated hornets, then ceased.

The chorus of echoing detonations subsided gradually. After a few minutes, Fargo moved out of the niche and resumed his climb to the canyon rim. He moved now with infinite care, testing each handhold carefully before calling upon it to support his full weight. He did not so much climb as insinuate his way up the steep slope like an enormous worm, seeking every ridge, taking advantage of each outcropping of rock, pulling himself relentlessly higher and higher.

He was within fifteen yards of the rim when he heard the chink of spurs and Ringo's sullen voice snap an order to Daisy. Now, he realized, while Ringo was distracted by Daisy, would be a good time for Fargo to charge up the rest of the slope. The incline from Fargo's present position to the rim was not as steep as that which he had already negotiated. But the angle of incline was not the problem. As Fargo made this last dash to the crest, he would be moving across a brow of open rock and would be entirely exposed all the way.

Still, it was too late to go back now. Unholstering his Colt, Fargo pushed himself from behind cover and started to race across the rock face. He had already removed his spurs and his passage across the smooth rock was reasonably quiet, but in the canyon's awesome silence, the rapid thud of his boots striking the rock's surface began to echo significantly.

He kept going and burst over the rim. Ringo was crouching, waiting. He had planted Daisy just in front of him. Fargo did not dare fire. This close in, Ringo had put aside his rifle. As Fargo raced toward him, Ringo's six-gun spat. Fargo felt his hat lift from his head as he flung himself to the ground and rolled to one side for cover.

A bullet struck the rock wall beside him. Tiny fragments of stone dug into his eyes. Fargo twisted his head away, then took cover behind a large boulder and waited for his chance to return Ringo's fire.

He heard the hammer of Ringo's six-gun come down on an empty chamber. Glancing around the boulder, Fargo saw Ringo bolting back along the canyon rim. And he had left Daisy behind.

Fargo darted out from behind the boulder and raced after Ringo, Daisy scrambling after him. Fargo pulled up suddenly. Ringo had trapped himself on a trail above them that led nowhere. He was now in full sight, crouching beside a great boulder, frantically reloading his six-gun.

Fargo shoved Daisy behind a boulder, then called up to Ringo. "Drop that iron, Ringo!"

Ringo stopped reloading his revolver. Slowly, carefully, he stood up. "All right, Fargo. You got me cold. I give up. I'm going to throw my six-gun to you and come on down there. You wouldn't shoot an unarmed man, would you?"

Fargo did not reply.

Taking Fargo's silence as assent, Ringo threw his six-gun down the trail. It clattered to a halt at Fargo's feet. Fargo kicked it off the canyon rim.

"All right," Fargo said to Ringo. "Come on down here."

As Fargo kept his six-gun trained on his chest, Johnny Ringo picked his way slowly down the narrow trail toward them.

"Fargo," said Daisy angrily, her voice hard. "I don't trust him."

Pulling up in front of them, Ringo smiled at the girl. "Why, Daisy! Don't be so nervous! What could I do now? Fargo's got me plumb licked."

Fargo stepped back and glanced in Daisy's direction and asked her to retrieve his hat for him. That momentary lapse was all Ringo had been waiting for. He lunged suddenly at Fargo.

Fargo tried to bring up his Colt. But Ringo's lowered head and shoulder struck Fargo in the chest, slamming him back against a rock face. Dazed, Fargo felt his Colt clatter to the ground. He shoved Ringo roughly back. But by this time Ringo had pulled a bowie from his shirt and was lunging at Fargo a second time.

Fargo managed to slip to one side as the blade flashed down. He felt a sharp pain in his shoulder, but ignored it as he reached up and caught Ringo's right wrist with both hands, then twisted. Ringo gasped, then cried out. The bowie clattered to the trail. Ignoring Johnny Ringo's other fist beating at him frantically, Fargo simply kept on twisting. The wrist snapped—as loudly as a piece of dry firewood.

Fargo released Ringo and stepped back.

His face a white mask of pain, Ringo stood swaying before them, clasping his shattered wrist with his left hand. He looked as if he might pass out at any moment. Daisy, meanwhile, had retrieved Fargo's rifle. Now she pointed it at Ringo, her trigger finger coiled about the trigger, a cool, calculating mask of hate on her face. There was no doubt what she intended. As Ringo cringed suddenly back, Fargo turned to her.

"Don't, Daisy. Let me have that."

She hesitated a moment, then reluctantly handed the rifle to Fargo.

"That's right," Ringo panted. "You can't kill me like that. Besides, Fargo, you don't have a warrant for my arrest. All you have is that damned badge.

You're not even a law officer. You got no right to hold me! Neither of you have."

"Maybe you're right," admitted Fargo.

"Fargo!" Daisy cried. "You can't mean that! Not after what he and that Indian did to Ike!"

Fargo turned to her. "Ringo's right, Daisy. All I have is this badge. And I don't have a warrant." Fargo looked back at Ringo and smiled. "Legally, Ringo, you can't be punished for that raise, not in this territory. You'd only go free if I brought you in to Clay Springs—or any other jurisdiction in this territory."

"See that," Ringo cried, a glint of hope springing into his eyes. "You can't arrest me. It won't be legal!"

Fargo nodded, smiling. "That's right, Ringo. And seeing I can't legally arrest you, it looks like I'll just have to finish you right here. If there ain't a court in the West that would convict you, I don't figure I have any choice in the matter." Lifting his rifle, Fargo took a step back.

"Hey, now wait a minute!" cried Ringo. "You don't mean that! Remember! I saved your life! I could've killed you back there. Instead I gave you a chance with them two prospectors."

"That was your mistake, Johnny."

Fargo flipped off the rifle's safety catch.

With a desperate cry, Ringo turned and started to run. Fargo fired at the trail in front of Ringo to rattle him, then flung aside the empty rifle. Snatching up his Colt, he fired again at Ringo, this round ricocheting off a rock wall inches from Ringo's head.

In a panic, Johnny Ringo swerved and tried to cut

up a narrow trail. But in his haste, he ran too close to the canyon rim. He stumbled, then caught himself for a moment before his feet began to slide backward on the gravel. One foot slipped out over the edge. He reached out to grab a boulder, but his shattered wrist made that impossible as he flinched away in pain. He flung out his other hand, but it was already too late as both feet now flew out from under him. His good left hand grabbed a small, gnarled bush, but it came out by the roots.

With a scream Ringo disappeared over the edge.

His scream was cut off quickly—too quickly, in fact.

Fargo and Daisy peered over the rim and saw Johnny Ringo lying on his back on a narrow outcropping about twenty yards below them. He was in full view, lying on his back. A thin trickle of blood was running from one corner of his mouth.

"I can't move, Fargo!" he cried. "My back! It's broke! I landed on something sharp!"

"It's another trick," said Daisy.

"I don't think so," Fargo said. Then he shouted down to Ringo, "Try to move!"

Fargo watched the man closely. It was obvious Ringo was struggling to make some kind of movement, but he lay as still as a gold piece.

Gasping, Ringo cried, "I tell you, I can't move! Not an inch. I got no feeling from the neck down! You got to get me out of here!"

"No," Fargo replied coldly. "You're too far down. There's no way we can get down to you in time."

"For the love of God! Don't leave me like this!"

"I don't have any choice."

Suddenly the shadow of a buzzard passed between them and the sun. For a split second it darkened Johnny Ringo. Fargo glanced up at it. This creature would be the first of many before the day was out.

Glancing up at the buzzard also, Daisy murmured, "Good."

Fargo knew what she was thinking. Vultures did not drop upon carrion because they smelled death, as so many thought. It was in reality their sharp eyes that detected any carcass—a dead steer or a dead human—that lay in the sun for hours without protection. Soon other buzzards would join the one up there now, and after a while they would alight on the ledge beside Ringo. Ringo would scream, but he would not be able to move—and before long, while he still lived, the buzzards' tearing beaks would begin slicing into his still-warm flesh. . . .

Fargo checked his Colt's load, then aimed carefully down at Ringo.

"No!" Daisy cried, when she saw what he was about to do. "Let him be! Let the vultures pick him apart while the son of a bitch is still alive! It's what he deserves!"

Ignoring her, Fargo thumbcocked his weapon and took careful aim on Johnny Ringo's swarthy face. Without protest, Ringo peered up at him and swallowed. He had heard Daisy's words and from where he lay, he could see as clearly as Fargo and Daisy the circling buzzard. He knew what Fargo was going to do—and why.

"Make it a clean shot, you son of a bitch," he called.

"I'll do what I can," Fargo promised.

The knife wound in Fargo's left shoulder caused him to flinch slightly an instant before he pulled the trigger, but it did not destroy his aim. Daisy turned away, then covered her face with her hands. Fargo holstered his Colt, then pulled his badge from his pocket and tossed it into the canyon. Its hold on him was gone now—forever.

He turned to Daisy. She was weeping silently. "It's over," he told her.

She nodded and wiped her eyes.

He put his arms about her shoulders and pulled her gently close. "I think maybe we better go back to Ike's place to rest up," he told her. "It'll be safe enough. For a while, anyway. I heard the Crows are pulling out."

She leaned her head wearily against his shoulder. "Yes," she said. "Let's do that. It's what I need."

He corrected her gently. "It's what we both need."

Fargo stood naked before the window, a bright stripe of moonlight across his solid chest, Daisy's fresh bandage neatly encasing his shoulder. He had awakened from a deep sleep, thinking of Ike—the big crooked mountain man gone forever in the flames of Tarnell's ranch. Ike had had a Viking funeral and there had been plenty of dogs at his feet.

From behind him came the sound of Daisy's silken limbs stirring under the sheets. Then came the soft pad of her naked footsteps on the wooden floor behind him. Her cool arms closed about him

169

and he felt her rest her cheek gently against his back.

"Can't sleep?" she asked softly.

"Just woke up."

"Mmm, your body is so warm."

Chuckling softly, he turned and looked down into her face, a pale oval in the moonlight. He could barely make out the faint sprinkling of freckles across her cheeks. For a girl with freckles, she was a pulsing, exploding revelation in a man's arms. Stepping boldly against his nakedness, she pressed her muff against his lifting manhood. Then she flung her hands around his neck and leaned back, grinding mischievously into him, her eyes gleaming.

"Come back to bed," she said.

"Yes."

He bent swiftly, caught her thighs, and lifted her easily into his arms. As he carried her to the bed, she bent forward and pressed her face into the crook of his neck, her mouth fastening to his skin, her tongue flicking it lightly. He let her down on the bed and dropped beside her, his face pressing into the warmth of her large, pear-shaped breasts. She stroked his hair gently as she hugged him to her.

Then slowly he shifted her under him on the bed and knelt over her, grinning suddenly down at her.

"Again?" she asked softly.

He nodded. "Makes a man forget the bad things," he told her.

She closed her hands about his neck and drew his lips down to hers. The kiss was long and wanton, transforming the glow in his loins to a hot, lancing fire. Then she lay back and stirred lasciviously under him, her hand reaching down.

"For a woman, too," she said.

They had little more to do with words after that. They let their bodies do the talking.

LOOKING FORWARD!

The following is the opening section
from the next novel in the exciting
Trailsman series from Signet:

THE TRAILSMAN #37: VALLEY OF DEATH

*The Utah territory, 1861, just below Black Canyon,
where law and order are only words that come
at the end of a six-gun . . .*

"You can't hang that man."

Judge Samuel Tolliver's long face grew red as he fastened watery-blue eyes on the big man with the chiseled face in the center of his makeshift courtroom. "Are you telling me who I can hang and who I can't hang, mister?" he roared.

"I'm saying this man is innocent and I don't expect you'd want to hang an innocent man," the big man answered calmly. His lake-blue eyes took in the frayed collar of Judge Tolliver's black frock coat, the stained lapels, and the starched shirt collar that had long lost its stiffness. He'd seen judges like this one before, in other little makeshift courtrooms as seedy as this one—men bought, paid for, and owned. But then, Owl Creek was a seedy little excuse for a town.

"You saying you want to testify in this here trial, mister?" he heard Judge Tolliver ask.

"Yes, sir, your Honor," the big man said as he pulled his powerful, hard-muscled figure to its feet.

Judge Tolliver's long face grew more sour than usual. "Step up and speak your piece," he muttered. "You swear to tell the truth and nothing else?"

"I swear," the big man said as he stepped forward.

"You've got a name? Let's have it," the judge barked.

"Fargo," the man with the lake-blue eyes said. "Skye Fargo."

He saw Judge Tolliver's eyes narrow as he exchanged glances with a thickset man in the first row of chairs, wearing a sheriff's badge on his shirt. The judge brought his eyes back to Fargo. "Heard the name," he commented. "You the one they call the Trailsman?" Fargo nodded. "What are you doing in these parts?" the judge asked.

"Passing through," Fargo said. "I saw that barn on fire last night, heard the horses screaming inside. I rode down to try to do something, but the fire was too big by the time I got there."

"So you saw the fire. That doesn't mean Tom Hanford didn't set it like Sheriff Curry says he did," the judge snapped.

Fargo's quiet calm stayed unruffled. "The sheriff

says he did it alone, that he had a grudge against this man Lansing. I saw four men high-tailing it away from the fire. That man wasn't one of them," he said, nodding toward the small, slightly round-shouldered man seated beside a sheriff's deputy.

"Maybe you saw wrong," Judge Tolliver said, his long face dyspeptic.

"Maybe you hear wrong," Fargo returned coldly. "Four men. Four," he repeated.

Again, Judge Tolliver's watery eyes exchanged a glance with the sheriff before returning to the big man before him. "All right, mister, you've said your piece. I call a fifteen-minute recess in this here trial."

He rose, frayed black frock coattails flapping behind him as he hurried into an adjoining room and pulled the door closed after him. Fargo returned to his seat and saw the sheriff rise and start to push his way through the spectators. The man's eyes, hard gray, paused for a moment on the big man with the handsome, chiseled face, and then he hurried out. Sheriff Curry was a bigger man than he appeared sitting down, Fargo noted, heavy, barrel chest and a thick neck, a block face with small features: short nose, tight mouth, and squinty eyes. Fargo's eyes moved across the crowded little room to halt at the girl across the way from him. Hands clenched in her lap, shoulders held stiffly pulled back, she looked taut as a steel wire, but fresh and pretty at the same time.

Fargo released a long sigh. He'd come upon her

only twenty-four hours ago and here he was in this dreary little courtroom. His silent snort was a derisive comment. Doing good deeds was like chasing tumbleweed: you never knew where it'd take you. Only damn fools bothered to do either. But then everybody has to be a damn fool once in a while, he smiled inwardly. The little courtroom hummed with the murmur of conversation and Fargo let his eyes half-close, his thoughts wind backward.

It had been almost noon, the sun high, as he edged his Ovaro along a ridge thick with black oak and paper birch. He'd seen the three men and the girl ride into sight through the trees, moving along open land a dozen yards below where he rode. The girl's voice drifted up to him clearly, words of anger and accusation. "You won't get away with it, damn you," she said, and Fargo reined up to peer through the trees. She had short-cut brown hair, a little turned-up nose, and a wide mouth that combined to give her a pugnacious kind of prettiness. He was too far away to see the color of her eyes, but he could see round, high breasts that filled the off-white shirt she wore. As he watched, the three men drew to a halt.

"Get off the horse, bitch," he heard one rasp, and he saw a deputy sheriff's badge on his buckskin jacket. "Roy said to teach you a lesson, and we're gonna do it here and now."

"Roy Curry's a rotten, no-good bastard and you're no better. You leave me alone," the girl flung back. She started to spur the horse on, but one of the men moved in quickly and caught the animal by the cheek strap. Fargo watched the other two dismount and reach for the girl. She kicked out, and one, a long, thin, spidery man, ducked away from a boot that grazed his face.

"Goddamn," he swore as he picked himself up from the ground. The girl tried to back the horse free, but the third man kept his grip. She turned as another of the men reached for her and she kicked out again. But the spidery-legged one had come around the other side and Fargo saw him grasp one of her legs and yank hard. She flew from the saddle and he grabbed her as the one with the badge came around to help him.

"Bastards," the girl shouted as she struggled, but they kept their grip and dragged her around to the other side of the horse.

"Tie her to that sapling over there," the deputy sheriff ordered, and Fargo continued to watch as the girl, cursing and kicking, was dragged and tied to the young tree, her arms stretched around the trunk so that her face pressed against the bark.

"Roy said to see you didn't come back making trouble again," the one with the badge snarled as he took a bullwhip from his saddle.

Fargo grimaced as he edged the Ovaro down through the trees. He didn't know what this was all about and he didn't like interfering in things he didn't know about. But he didn't much like what he was seeing, either, and he steered the Ovaro down the sharp slope.

"Lift that shirt up," the deputy called, and the spidery-legged man yanked the girl's shirt up half over her head. Fargo saw a tanned, young, firm-skinned, strong back and the lovely edge of one high breast. The man snapped the bullwhip as he laughed. "You're gonna be sorry you always been so goddamn high and mighty with me, honey. I'm gonna enjoy whipping your butt," he said.

Fargo moved the Ovaro into the open while the three men still had their backs to him, intent on what they were going to do. The man with the bullwhip raised his arm to send the whip lashing out. "Hold it right there, mister," Fargo said quietly, and the trio whirled in surprise. The one holding the bullwhip kept his arm upraised.

"Who the hell are you?" He frowned.

"Doesn't matter. Just drop the whip," Fargo said.

The man's mouth curled into a snarling sneer. "You come to rescue the little lady, cowboy?" he asked.

"Guess so," Fargo said.

"Well, you can guess again. You've got three seconds to get your dumb ass out of my sight," the man snarled.

"Untie the girl," Fargo said calmly.

The man's frown deepened. "Maybe you didn't hear me, cowboy," he said.

"I heard you. Untie the girl," Fargo answered.

"There are three of us here. You crazy?" the man said.

"Either that or maybe I can't count," Fargo said

softly. He smiled inwardly as he saw the three men glance at each other. He knew what they were thinking: no man took on three guns unless he was damn sure of himself or a damn fool, and they didn't see a damn fool in the ice-blue of his eyes. Fargo saw the deputy's wrist go backward, his shoulder tighten as he started to send the bullwhip lashing out. Fargo's hand moved and the big Colt .45 seemed to fly from its holster and fire all in one motion. The shot creased the man's hand and he roared in pain as the bullwhip flew from his grasp.

"Jesus," he said as he half-turned and pressed the side of his hand to his shirt.

Fargo's eyes flicked to the other two men. He saw the spidery-legged one swallow hard as the third one remained motionless. "Mount up and move out," Fargo said.

The deputy spit back angry words as he tied a kerchief around his hand. "I see you again I'll put daylight through you," he said with a bravado not echoed in his eyes. "Besides, you're interfering with official business. She's my prisoner."

"He's a damn liar. I'm nobody's prisoner," the girl called out.

"I got orders to see she didn't come back to town," the man said.

"You just got new orders. Get your ass out of here," Fargo said.

The man started to pull himself on his horse, the other two following. "We've a score to settle, mister," the deputy growled.

"Whenever you want," Fargo said. "Order yourself a pine box first."

The man glared and turned his horse away to ride off at a fast trot with his two companions.

Fargo watched till he was satisfied they weren't returning, and then he strode to the girl. She wriggled her torso and the shirt tumbled down as he reached her. He untied her wrist bonds and saw her eyes search his face, take in the chiseled handsomeness, the black brows. Light-brown, round eyes, he noted. They were wide, frank, and fit the pugnacious prettiness of her.

"I owe you," she said. "That bullwhip would've cut me up real bad. I'm Bess Hanford."

"Fargo . . . Skye Fargo," the Trailsman replied. "What was that all about?"

"My pa," she snapped angrily. "He's in Sheriff Curry's jail for burning down Dorrance Lansing's barn and killing three horses." Her eyes flashed brown flame. "It's a lie, of course, one more piece of railroading. Only worse. My pa won't give in like the others."

"The others?" Fargo inquired as he walked beside her to her horse, a solid brown mare with a hint of Morgan in her, he noted.

"My pa's not the first. But it was only a matter of time before Dorrance Lansing got to us. He's cleared most everybody out of the valley," Bess Hanford said, and her voice was suddenly flat and filled with dejection, her pretty face turned dark and grave. She halted beside her horse, and her light-brown eyes studied him again. "It takes some telling. If you've a mind to hear, come with me. I'll fix you a good supper while we talk," she offered.

"Why not?" He shrugged. A good meal and a pretty girl were a lot better than beef jerky and wandering coyotes. He'd come near Owl Creek following a lead that hadn't held up. But then most of them didn't. Yet he never turned away from any. He couldn't, any more than a starving man can turn away from food. That day when they'd murdered his family was written in his blood. It would only be erased when he'd caught the last two of the murdering gang. They were out there, a debt waiting to be collected. Someplace, somewhere, sometime, he'd find them, just as he had the others.

He turned and pulled himself onto the Ovaro as Bess Hanford rode off. She had a round little rear that filled the riding britches and she rode with a good, steady hand, he saw. They'd gone but a mile or so into a long, lush valley when she turned and led the way to a small house with a stable and hog pens to one side. Fargo saw at least twenty hogs in clean pens and, behind them, rows of tilled soil. He followed Bess into the stable and unsaddled the Ovaro. "Got good pork chops waiting for tonight, best you'll ever taste," she told him pridefully.

"Must be your own stock." He grinned, and she nodded as she led him into the house. A wide and spacious room made the house seem larger than it had from outside. A long, worn green sofa rested on a frayed rug, and the room opened onto a kitchen with an open space between that was hung with kettles and iron skillets. Bess gestured to the long green sofa as she opened a corner cabinet and brought out a burlap-covered jug.

"Good sippin' whiskey," she said as she poured a glass for him and one for herself. "Set down while I set the fire to burning," she said, and he folded his long frame onto the sofa and took a slow pull on the whiskey. She'd been right, he murmured. It was good, full-bodied rye. His eyes watched her as she came back into the room. No sensuous gliding walk for Bess Hanford, he observed: she moved with quick, energetic, bouncy steps that made her jiggle in all the right places. She slid down beside him and her pert face grew solemn at once as she sipped the whiskey. "About Dorrance Lansing," she began. "He wants the land in this valley and he's rich enough to do anything to get it. He's behind everything that's happened."

"Just what's that?" Fargo asked.

"Almost everyone in the valley has been framed by Dorrance Lansing and cheated out of their lands. He uses a jackal of a sheriff and a hyena of a judge."

"How do they frame people?" Fargo questioned.

"They see that someone gets into an argument with Lansing or one of his men. Next thing, something happens and they frame one of the valley people for it, the way they've framed my pa for burning down Lansing's barn," Bess said, and took a long pull of the whiskey. "They'll give him the same choice they gave the others, hanging or clearing out, leaving their land."

"For this Dorrance Lansing to pick up," Fargo said.

"Exactly," Bess Hanford bit out. "Naturally, clearing out is better than hanging to most people."

"Most?" Fargo frowned.

"Bill Stebbins wouldn't give in. I always felt he thought they'd never go all the way, even when that rotten judge sentenced him. But he was wrong. They hung him just the way they'll hang my pa," Bess said, and Fargo's brows lifted in question. "Pa won't give in, either. He won't clear out. He's told me so. They can hang him, but I'll still have the land, he said."

"Till they come after you," Fargo said.

"That's what I've tried to tell him, but Pa's a stubborn man. We have to stand up to them, no matter what. He's always believed in principles. They're saying he did it all on his own. They'll sentence him and hang him for it."

"No, they won't," Fargo said.

Bess Hanford's hand came out—a quick, impulsive gesture—touched his arm, and pulled away at once. "I thank you for trying to make me feel better, but there's no use," she said as she finished her drink.

"I saw the barn go up in flames and I saw four men ride away from it," Fargo said, and watched her eyes widen.

"You saw it?" she gasped.

"And I'll tell the judge what I saw," Fargo said. She flung herself against him, her arms curling around his neck, and he felt the soft pressure of her breasts, the warm sweetness of her around him before she pulled back quickly. He saw the hope fade from her face even as he watched.

"I owe you again, for wanting to help," she said. "But it won't work. They'll hang him."

"No judge can ignore an eyewitness," Fargo said.

"They'll find a way," Bess said glumly.

"They can't," Fargo told her. "Now you just stop being so damn sure things will go wrong."

Her smile was sudden and sad, full of wry wisdom. "Thanks for being so sure things will go right," she said. She leaned forward, brushed his lips with hers, pulled away quickly.

"You offering me passion or pork chops?" He grinned.

Her light-brown eyes grew thoughtful. "Pork chops. For now," she said.

"That'll do," he told her. "For now."

She rose and he watched her retreat into the kitchen, plump, rounded rear bouncing deliciously. Bess Hanford's pert prettiness, her open, frank honesty, set her apart from most women, he decided. No guile, no coyness to her, but a directness that was its own kind of sensuousness.

"Help yourself to another drink," she called from the kitchen, and he took the offer and sat back to enjoy the warmth of the whiskey as it curled itself inside him. When Bess called again, it was for supper; she served a hearty meal on a pine table at one side of the kitchen: thick pork chops, corn bread, and collard greens. When they finished, she turned the lamp on in the main room and folded herself on the worn green sofa next to him to sip on another glass of whiskey. The top buttons on her shirt had come open and he enjoyed the smooth, round curve of one high breast as she sat back.

"The pork chops were damn good," Fargo said. "I'm wondering if the passion's goin' to match."

Her light-brown eyes met the laughter in his glance with quiet seriousness. "You'll not be finding out tonight," she said. "I'm not for saying thanks that way. You ought to be hungry, not grateful, when you go to a man, I've always felt."

"Couldn't agree more," Fargo said. "You saying you're not hungry?"

She remained quietly thoughtful. "I'm saying I'm not ready. There's a difference," she answered.

"There is," he agreed. "I'm in no special hurry. I think you'd be worth waiting for, Bess Hanford."

"Compliments on top of rescuin'?" she said. "You go around the country doing just that?"

"Not usually," he laughed. "They call me the Trailsman."

Her light-brown eyes stayed on him, a long, studying stare. "I'm thinking you read people as well as trails," Bess said.

"One goes with the other," he told her.

"Anyway, I'm beholden to you for helping me today and for trying to help Pa tomorrow," Bess

Hanford said, her pert face staying sober as she rose to her feet. "We've an extra room with a good cot in it. It's yours for the night," she said.

"Good enough," he said, and got to his feet as she lit a hurricane lamp and led the way to the room. It had a single window half-open, a washstand and big white porcelain pitcher, a cot and a three-legged puncheon table beside it.

"Sleep well, Fargo," she said.

"You, too," he said, and watched her pull the door closed after her as she left. He undressed to his shorts and turned off the little lamp. The cot was six inches too short for him, but it was firmly comfortable and he relaxed and let thoughts drift idly through his mind. There were questions he hadn't asked of Bess, questions he wasn't sure he wanted to pursue. Taking her pa out of a hangman's noose was one thing. Getting involved in a land feud was something else. He'd be content to settle for the first, he mused silently, and maybe wait to see if Bess Hanford could get herself hungry enough or ready enough. He closed his eyes and let sleep come with the warm wind that sifted in through the half-open window.

He'd been asleep for at least three hours, he guessed, when his mountain cat's hearing woke him, the sound hardly more than a soft murmur. But the sound was the unmistakable rattle of a rein chain, and the whinny of a horse drifted into the little room. Fargo was on his feet at once, pulling on trousers and gun belt. One long stride took him to the window, where, peering out into the night, he saw Bess emerging from the stable, pulling the brown mare behind her. He had on boots and was out of the house as she began to swing into the saddle. "Where in hell are you going?" he growled as he took hold of the mare's headstall.

Bess frowned, first in surprise, then in determination. "To get my pa out of jail," she said.

"You mean to get yourself shot," Fargo said.

"No, I'll get him out. I'll find a way," she insisted.

"Dammit, I told you I'd tell them what I saw, come morning." Fargo frowned back.

"And I told you they'll get around that," she said.

"They want to make everything look lawful. They can't do that and ignore an eyewitness," he told her.

"You don't know them," she said. "I'm getting him out of there tonight."

"Hell you are. I didn't save your hide from being bullwhipped so's you could get it shot full of holes," Fargo flung at her. "And that's sure as hell what'll happen if you go charging into that jail." She didn't answer, but the stubborn anger stayed in her eyes. "You getting off that horse or do I take you off?" he said.

Her answer was a quick pull on the reins that yanked the mare's head around and tore her away from his grip on the headstall. Bess slapped the mare on the rump and the horse started to leap forward, but Fargo dived, one arm swinging out to encircle the girl's waist. He yanked and she flew from the saddle as the mare went forward. He caught her in his arms as she struggled and tried to punch at him.

"Dammit, you let me go," she hissed.

"When you stop being a little fool," he told her as he lifted and carried her into the house. He saw the bedroom door was open, entered the room, and tossed her onto the bed, where she bounced once and came to a stop. He saw tears held back in her eyes as she glared at him.

"You don't know them. They won't listen to you," she shouted.

"They'll have to," he said. "You breaking your pa out of jail will only make it worse for him, even if you got lucky and pulled it off."

She rocked back and forth on her knees, her eyes closed. "You don't know them, you just don't know them," she chanted.

"Do I have to tie you up for the rest of the night?" he said, and she snapped her eyes open to peer at him.

"You wouldn't do that," she muttered. "Yes, you would," she corrected herself. "No, you don't have to do that," she said.

"I've your word you won't pull any more stunts like that one?" he pressed. She didn't answer and he kicked the door shut with his knee. "All right, there's not too much of the night left. I'll just bed down here. You make one move and I'll hear it," he said. He moved to the edge of the big double bed that took up most of the room, and pale moonlight affording just enough light to see, he pulled off gun belt and trousers and lay down on the bed in his shorts. Hands behind his head, he stretched and felt his powerful muscles ripple down his hard-packed frame. Bess hadn't moved as she watched him. "You won't be getting much sleeping sitting on your knees that way," he said casually.

"I won't be sleeping any," she snapped, but she pulled herself up, swung her body around, and lay down on the other side of the bed.

"Suit yourself," he said, and he closed his eyes to tiny slits that let him barely see her as she lay on her back, high, very round breasts pushing almost straight upward. He lay that way, feigning sleep, and saw her turn her head to peer curiously at him. He watched as her eyes traveled up and down his body until finally she turned her back to him and settled herself on the pillow. He let sleep come to him, then. He snapped awake three times during the remainder of the night, but she was only turning fitfully on her side of the bed.

When morning came, he woke to look across at her. Sleep had refused denial and she lay with her eyes closed, her lips slightly parted, pert little face slightly stubborn even in sleep. He rose, pulled on trousers, gun belt, and boots, and silently went into the extra room to finish. Finally washed and dressed, he woke her gently.

She turned and sat up, startled, the middle button of her shirt popping open to let him glimpse the very round, tanned smoothness of one breast. She pulled the blouse closed at once, her frown instant as she pushed herself from the bed.

"I'll be out in a minute," she muttered crossly.

"I'll saddle up," he said. He left for the stable and had just finished saddling the Ovaro when she appeared, her eyes wide as she looked at him.

"You were wrong last night," she muttered. "You shouldn't have stopped me. You meant well, I know that, but you were wrong."

"You were wrong," he said sharply. "Now let's get to town. I want to speak my piece and get this done with."

Fargo's half-closed eyes snapped open, ending his drifting thoughts as the door slammed and he saw Judge Samuel Tolliver striding to his chair behind the makeshift bench. Black frock coattails trailing behind his long, spindly figure, he looked not unlike a tattered crow, Fargo reflected. The judge banged his gavel on the bench.

"Court's in session," he proclaimed. "It's time to decide this here case."

JOIN THE *TRAILSMAN* READERS' PANEL

Help us bring you more of the books you like by filling out this survey and mailing it in today.

1. Book Title: _____

   Book #: _____

2. Using the scale below, how would you rate this book on the following features? Please write in one rating from 0-10 for each feature in the spaces provided.

POOR		NOT SO GOOD			O.K.		GOOD		EXCEL- LENT	
0	1	2	3	4	5	6	7	8	9	10

RATING

Overall opinion of book .... _____
Plot/Story .... _____
Setting/Location .... _____
Writing Style .... _____
Character Development .... _____
Conclusion/Ending .... _____
Scene on Front Cover .... _____

3. About how many western books do you buy for yourself each month? _____

4. How would you classify yourself as a reader of westerns? I am a ( ) light ( ) medium ( ) heavy reader.

5. What is your education?
   ( ) High School (or less)   ( ) 4 yrs. college
   ( ) 2 yrs. college   ( ) Post Graduate

6. Age _____   7. Sex: ( ) Male ( ) Female

Please Print Name_____

Address_____

City _____ State _____ Zip _____

Phone # ( )_____

Thank you. Please send to New American Library, Research Dept., 1633 Broadway, New York, NY 10019.

Exciting Westerns by Jon Sharpe from SIGNET

(0451)

☐ THE TRAILSMAN #1: SEVEN WAGONS WEST   (127293—$2.50)*
☐ THE TRAILSMAN #2: THE HANGING TRAIL   (110536—$2.25)
☐ THE TRAILSMAN #3: MOUNTAIN MAN KILL   (121007—$2.50)*
☐ THE TRAILSMAN #4: THE SUNDOWN SEARCHERS   (122003—$2.50)*
☐ THE TRAILSMAN #5: THE RIVER RAIDERS   (127188—$2.50)*
☐ THE TRAILSMAN #6: DAKOTA WILD   (119886—$2.50)*
☐ THE TRAILSMAN #7: WOLF COUNTRY   (123697—$2.50)
☐ THE TRAILSMAN #8: SIX-GUN DRIVE   (121724—$2.50)*
☐ THE TRAILSMAN #9: DEAD MAN'S SADDLE   (126629—$2.50)*
☐ THE TRAILSMAN #10: SLAVE HUNTER   (114655—$2.25)
☐ THE TRAILSMAN #11: MONTANA MAIDEN   (116321—$2.25)
☐ THE TRAILSMAN #12: CONDOR PASS   (118375—$2.50)*
☐ THE TRAILSMAN #13: BLOOD CHASE   (119274—$2.50)*
☐ THE TRAILSMAN #14: ARROWHEAD TERRITORY   (120809—$2.50)*
☐ THE TRAILSMAN #15: THE STALKING HORSE   (121430—$2.50)*
☐ THE TRAILSMAN #16: SAVAGE SHOWDOWN   (122496—$2.50)*
☐ THE TRAILSMAN #17: RIDE THE WILD SHADOW   (122801—$2.50)*
☐ THE TRAILSMAN #18: CRY THE CHEYENNE   (123433—$2.50)*

*Price is $2.95 in Canada

Buy them at your local

bookstore or use coupon

on next page for ordering.

Wild Westerns by Warren T. Longtree